A blast

"Sean?!"

TJ's face blanched, and her eyes widened in recognition.

Sean gripped her arms to keep her from falling. Her knees shook as if she was about to drop to the floor in a dead faint, or so he told himself as he pulled her against his chest.

The scent of spring flowers wafted beneath his nose, sending him back to Dindi and the hotel suite he'd shared with this beautiful woman. For a long moment he allowed the good memories to wash over him. He wanted to continue holding her close until he recaptured that feeling of belonging he'd only experienced with her in that faraway room.

But the good feelings were chased away by bad memories. The blinding flash of the explosion and the resulting blackness filled his mind....

ELLE JAMES

BLOWN AWAY

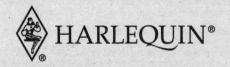

HARLEQUIN®

TORONTO • NEW YORK • LONDON
AMSTERDAM • PARIS • SYDNEY • HAMBURG
STOCKHOLM • ATHENS • TOKYO • MILAN • MADRID
PRAGUE • WARSAW • BUDAPEST • AUCKLAND

This book is dedicated to my friends Stephen, Debbie,
Janelle, Brenna and Jenny for all their help with the
Washington, D.C., setting and the inner workings of the
Rayburn Building. Without your help, this book would
not have happened. Thank you!

ISBN-13: 978-0-373-69281-1
ISBN-10:   0-373-69281-1

BLOWN AWAY

ABOUT THE AUTHOR

Golden Heart Winner for Best Paranormal Romance of 2004, Elle James started writing when her sister issued the Y2K challenge to write a romance novel. She managed a full-time job, raised three wonderful children, and she and her husband even tried their hands at ranching exotic birds (ostriches, emus and rheas) in the Texas hill country. Ask her and she'll tell you what it's like to go toe-to-toe with an angry 350-pound bird! After leaving her successful career in information technology management, Elle is now pursuing her writing full-time. She loves building exciting stories about heroes, heroines, romance and passion. Elle loves to hear from fans. You can contact her at ellejames@earthlink.net or visit her Web site at www.ellejames.com.

Books by Elle James

HARLEQUIN INTRIGUE

906—BENEATH THE TEXAS MOON
938—DAKOTA MELTDOWN
961—LAKOTA BABY
987—COWBOY SANCTUARY
1014—BLOWN AWAY

CAST OF CHARACTERS

Sean McNeal—Stealth Operations Specialist (S.O.S.) who lost his focus, resulting in the loss of his partner. Going undercover, he's determined to find his partner's killer.

TJ Barton—Legislative analyst TJ loses her lover in an act of terrorism. But when she sees him again, is she suffering from posttraumatic stress syndrome, or is she seeing a ghost?

Congressman Thomas Crane—Pushing a funding program similar to the murdered Congressman Haddock. What does he have to gain?

Congresswoman Ann Malone—Driven congresswoman, determined to make it in a man's world of politics.

Gordon Harris—Dedicated legislative analyst to Congresswoman Ann Malone and in love with TJ.

Jason Frazier—Lobbyist for Midnight Oil Enterprises.

Royce Fontaine—Leader of the S.O.S. team.

Kat Sikes—Member of the S.O.S. team. Her husband, Marty, was killed in the line of duty.

Eddy Smith—He's connected to the mob, but was he responsible for Congressman Haddock's death?

Chapter One

Sean McNeal strode into the bedroom of the suite, a cup of coffee balanced in one hand. He stood for a moment enjoying the sight of legislative assistant Tessa Janine Barton sleeping. She insisted on being called TJ, reasoning that Tessa was too sweet, and she didn't consider herself sweet, although Sean disagreed.

Her chin-length sandy-blond hair spread out on the pillowcase in a semicircle and her cheeks were still flushed a rosy pink from making love into the small hours of the morning. The one thing he liked most about TJ was the intensity she applied to everything—her job, her politics and especially sex.

He'd known her only two weeks and, despite his vow to never let a woman sneak beneath the radar screen and clobber his defenses, he felt TJ had done just that. For the past few days Sean had been thinking dangerous thoughts of ever-after with one woman—a stream of consciousness he'd never swam up. TJ Barton with her athletic body, passion for life and ability to laugh just when you needed it most had slipped beneath his skin.

He'd fallen hard and rather than regret it, he woke each

morning looking forward to seeing her face on the pillow beside him. What would happen when they returned to the States and resumed their mutually disparate lives? Would he go back to being the perpetually single bachelor, utterly devoted to his job and nothing else?

Sean didn't want to think beyond today and TJ's beautiful body lying naked beneath the sheets. Rather than go to work, he wanted to yank off the tie strangling his throat, crawl out of the business suit he felt so alien in and get naked with her. Maybe spend the day in bed, recapturing the magic of last night's lovemaking.

Unfortunately, he had a job to do and so did she. He leaned over her and pressed a kiss to the erogenous zone behind her ear—that sensitive spot that drove her crazy. "Wake up, sleepyhead."

"Ummmm." She stretched, her lithe form outlined beneath the sheets. "What time is it?" Her voice was like soft gravel, a sexy whisper clouded with sleep.

"Your meeting begins in twenty minutes."

Her body halted in mid-stretch and her eyes flew open. "What?"

He really liked that her eyes were the deep brown of dark chocolate in stark contrast to her sandy-blond hair. "You have twenty minutes before you're expected at the embassy." He smacked her thigh. "Get up."

"Why didn't you wake me earlier?" She sat up, the sheet pooling around her waist, exposing the smooth skin and taut lines of her upper body and pert breasts.

"You looked so sexy, I hated to wake you. Besides, it's only a block to the embassy. If you hurry, you'll even have time for this cup of coffee." Truth was he'd felt guilty for keeping her up making love until two in the morning.

"Haddock will be furious if I'm not there on time." She flung the sheets aside and stood beside him.

Sean smoothed a hand down her hip and pulled her against him. "I'm all for skipping our meetings and staying here." Pressing a kiss to her lips, one hand slid up her back and the other down over her naked bottom.

"Ummm." Her tongue delved between his lips and dueled with his; her hands slipped beneath his jacket to wrap around his waist. She squeezed him hard and leaned back. "As interesting as the possibility sounds, I have to be there. Congressman Haddock is ready to wrap up this meeting with Dindian Prime Minister Abediayi and get back to the States." One more hard kiss and she pushed away.

Sean sighed. Back to the States. Back to the real world of high-paced metro living, where people barely had time to think much less get to know each other. "Does he still plan to leave the day after tomorrow?"

"If he can, he'd like to leave sooner," she said from the bathroom. "It all depends on the outcome of today's meeting. What about you?"

"My plans are fluid. I can come and go as I please, within reason."

"Must be nice to be your own boss." She strode back through the bedroom wearing a shell-pink bra and matching lace panties.

Sean resisted the urge to grab her and throw her on the bed. His business was her business, only he hadn't filled her in on all the details. In his line of work, the less everyone knew about his real job, the better. The outer shell he'd constructed was enough for anyone to know, including TJ.

As far as TJ Barton and personnel at the embassy were concerned, he was a business consultant there to assist the small African nation of Dindi with their application for assistance from the U.S. government through the Millennium Challenge program. His covert duty as a Stealth Operations Specialist was ferreting out insider information on Dindi and on terrorist activities purportedly sponsored by their president's opposing political party, or any other faction that could impact the congressman's visit.

He checked his watch. Marty Sikes expected him at the embassy in five minutes. "I need to go."

TJ zipped the back of her simple black skirt and padded over to him in bare feet. "Will I see you later?"

He nodded, staring down into her shining brown eyes. "Can't promise when."

"Me either." She stood on tiptoe and pressed a kiss to his lips. "I wish the day was already over."

"Same here." He returned the pressure, holding her close for only a moment more before he let go. The day ahead already seemed too long and he wasn't sure he liked feeling anxious to get through it.

"Sean?"

Pausing at the door, he turned toward her.

"This has been crazy, these last two weeks." One hand pushed her hair behind her ear, a habit she only displayed when she was nervous.

"Absolutely." Sean's gut knotted. He'd enjoyed the last two weeks, but was he ready to admit it meant more than just a fling?

She smiled, her face lighting the room. "I've had fun."

His belly flipped over that smile. "Same here."

Her lips straightened and her brow furrowed in that way he knew meant she was about to say something that meant a lot to her.

Recognizing and reading body language were all part of Sean's job. Sometimes he wished he wasn't so good at it. He found himself praying she wouldn't say anything declaratory, especially the L word. He'd never experienced love and he wasn't convinced it really existed. Even when he was a boy, that emotion was illusive. The only child of an alcoholic father, he hadn't known real affection. And his mother had split when he was barely five.

Nor was he certain he wanted the debilitating limitations involved with being in love. He'd watched his pal Marty go from a totally focused, leap-into-action S.O.S. agent to one who stopped to consider all his actions carefully before pursuing the one most reasonable and least life-threatening.

TJ pushed the hair behind her other ear. "When we go back to Washington—"

With his heart pounding against his ribs, Sean felt the sudden need to breathe open, fresh air, even in the smelly streets of Conbanau. He jerked the door open and said over his shoulder, "Let's cross that bridge when we get to it." And then he escaped like his life depended on it.

WHEN THE DOOR SLAMMED behind Sean, TJ shook her head. Okay, the guy wasn't ready for anything more than a fling. She'd suspected that was the case when he refused to open up about his past, his work or anything personal. Oh, he'd shared information about his favorite sports team and the foods he most enjoyed. But who was the real Sean McNeal? What made him tick? And why did he run when she'd only tried to mention a future beyond the two weeks they'd spent in Africa? She wouldn't ask for marriage or false promises. Heck, she hadn't even finished her sentence before he bolted.

She slipped her arms into the black silk jacket, glad of its lightweight fabric. The heat and humidity of the colorful coastal city of Conbanau could be oppressive as the day wore on. And today promised to be a very wearing day.

The thought that would get her through the long, boring meetings with the pompous prime minister and his mealymouthed financial aide was the knowledge that Sean would be somewhere in the embassy with her. And, if she hadn't scared him off, he'd be back in her room that night.

Her body tingled in anticipation and she peered out the window, catching sight of Sean crossing the busy street, dodging buses and brightly dressed men and women walking or riding bicycles. As he wove through the crowded streets to the embassy only a block away, his white skin and dark suit stood out in the sea of humanity. He wore his hair longer than most men, giving him a more daring look. The man was tall, dark, sexy and mysterious, making him everything she ever dreamed of, yet didn't have room for, in her life as a legislative assistant.

If she hadn't come to Dindi ahead of Congressman Haddock, she probably would never have met Sean at the little café between the hotel and the embassy. They would never have strolled along the beach at sunset talking about the stars and constellations. And they never would have captured the moonlight in that single, soul-defining kiss that launched them into a night of lovemaking unsurpassed by anything TJ had ever experienced.

She sighed, something she'd done a lot of in the past week. What was wrong with her? Her life was just as she loved it—fast-paced, exciting and purposeful. As a legislative assistant, she had more influence on government decisions than the average American. Since she'd left the FBI, she'd mentored with Mason Haddock, Republican congressman from the great state of Texas. Her work was safe, fascinating and everything she wanted.

Until Sean showed up. He was the icing on the cake. A businessman, not an FBI agent on a dangerous assignment. TJ liked that Sean wasn't in a career where dodging bullets was just another hazard of the job. She'd suffered through a relationship like that before and wanted nothing to do with danger and life-threatening situations. Give her safety and stability every day. She didn't miss the late-night stakeouts, being shot at by cornered criminals or waiting by the phone to hear if the man she thought she loved was dead or alive after a particularly dangerous assignment.

Granted, life as an FBI agent wasn't all shoot-outs and gunfire. They spent most of their time interviewing and digging through mounds of paperwork searching for clues. But all it took was one bullet, one bomb, one strung out junkie to ruin your day—or end a man's life.

No, sir. Give her a quiet government job where she could help shape decisions through intelligence instead of brute force. Although, sometimes she wanted to resort to brute force when the congressman was particularly stubborn on certain issues.

A quick glance at her watch made TJ gasp. Crud! Congressman Haddock would be furious if she wasn't there a full hour before the proposed meeting. Which gave her exactly four minutes to find her shoes and join the sea of people on the streets heading in the same direction as Sean.

Dashing back through the suite, she slipped into her serviceable black pumps, grabbed her briefcase and raced down the wide staircase of the five-star hotel. Atypical for the large African center of commerce, the streets were filled with people of all classes of society, each with a purpose for the day.

TJ's purpose was to get to the embassy in—she checked her watch—three minutes. Half walking and half running, she hurried down the long block toward the three-story, forty-five-room, sprawling U.S. embassy surrounded by an impressive wrought-iron fence and lush green lawns. She could see the building above the heads of the people surrounding her.

With his head start on her, Sean should be clearing the gate about now. She wished she'd woken when he had so that they could walk together and so she wouldn't be so winded when she arrived. As a legislative assistant, she prided herself in always being calm and collected. It was her job to make Congressman Haddock look good by being prepared and ready for anything and everything. Meeting Sean had thrown her into reactionary mode, constantly running to keep up.

As she neared the imposing building, the throng of people thinned. With the path clear, she was in the homestretch and should make it there only a few minutes after the congressman. TJ slowed short of the gate and dug in her purse for her passport and identification. When she found them she moved forward without looking up.

She bumped into a businessman leaving the gate at the same time as she approached. Her impression of the man was dark hair, intense brown eyes and an expensive pinstripe suit. TJ apologized for her clumsiness, but the businessman didn't even acknowledge her. He kept walking, his long strides eating the distance.

"Must be in a hurry." TJ showed her passport and government identification badge to the Marine standing guard. While she tucked the items back in her purse, Congressman Haddock's empty black limousine exited the compound. Great, he'd already arrived and was probably looking for her.

Slinging her purse back over her shoulder she'd taken two steps across the long, cobblestone drive when an explosion ripped through the air, knocking her off her feet and spewing stone, dust and debris across the green lawns.

The spacious white building with elegant arches crumbled before her eyes, the center collapsing into a pile of rubble. A cloud of black smoke and brown dust rose into the air, billowing out from the center of the blast.

TJ tried to sit up, but when she did, her ears rang and the scene before her spun out of control. Bending forward, she tucked her head between her knees, fighting for control of her senses and the contents of her stomach. When she managed to raise her head, her vision blurred, dust filled her lungs and she erupted in a burst of coughing.

Men and women ran toward a jumble of crumbled stone, jagged timbers and broken glass where the American embassy had once stood. People scrambled around the debris, but nothing moved beneath the destruction. Those who'd been inside couldn't have survived the blast.

Sean.

As the screech of sirens moved closer, a woman's wail rose above the noise. The sound emerged from deep in TJ's chest. She swayed, welcoming the black abyss dragging her into darkness.

Chapter Two

Spring in Washington, D.C. usually made TJ happy. Today, despite the blooming cherry blossoms, her jog was all work. She made her way through Rock Creek Park and down to the towpaths formerly used by the mules that towed barges along the Chesapeake and Ohio Canal. The C&O Canal ran parallel to the Potomac River and was usually a peaceful place to run. But TJ wasn't in a peaceful frame of mind.

A month had passed since Congressman Haddock's death and TJ's subsequent return from Conbanau. The government still didn't know much more about who caused the death and destruction. Several terrorist groups claimed responsibility, contradicting themselves and sending Congress, the CIA and the president into an uproar for resolution and vindication.

TJ had spent the week following the explosion helping the CIA and the American government with the investigation and arranging for the congressman's remains to be shipped back to the States. In between dodging reporters and trying to answer questions she didn't have the answers to, she searched for Sean.

All the surviving casualties had been sent to the Conbanau Mercy Hospital following the explosion. Although TJ insisted she was all right, they'd kept her overnight for observation. She'd managed to slip from her room and find Sean in the mass-casualty chaos the hospital staff was ill-prepared to handle.

Although his head was wrapped in a swath of white gauze bandages, he was the Sean she'd spent two wonderful weeks with. He'd been hooked up to IVs and was unconscious.

TJ wanted him to wake and talk to her, to hold her in his arms and tell her everything would be all right. But he was unresponsive, either due to his injuries or the drugs loaded into his IV. She sat beside him until a nurse chased her back to her room.

Sick over the death of Congressman Haddock, she'd crawled into her lone hospital bed and fallen into an exhausted sleep. She didn't wake until the nurse came through the following morning with breakfast.

TJ had waited until the nurse left the room and entered the next room down the hall. Then she slipped out to check on Sean.

When she reached the room she'd found him in the night before, another victim from the explosion occupied the bed Sean had been in.

As if in a fog, she checked the rooms on either side, afraid she'd been confused. Finally, she asked a nurse where Sean had been taken. The young woman checked her charts and then placed a hand on TJ's arm. That's when she was told Sean had been taken to the mortuary.

TJ stumbled on the path. Fewer people jogged on the dirt, choosing to keep their running shoes clean on the pavement. TJ preferred to be closer to the water and the relative solitude she could find in a city teeming with people.

The nightmares were only just beginning to fade and she liked to think she was getting her life back on track.

But then she'd gotten word from her contact in the CIA that the terrorist attack on the U.S. embassy hadn't been the responsibility of Prime Minister Abediayi's political opponents. Nor had it been any of the terrorist organizations claiming credit. The CIA suspected the death and destruction had been bought and paid for by an American citizen and they were digging into the case, more determined than ever to discover the organization or individual responsible.

Her mind had a hard time latching on to the news. An American had arranged for the explosion that killed Congressman Haddock, several legislative assistants, the American ambassador to Dindi and the Dindi prime minister, among too many others. The blast had also killed Sean McNeal, an innocent businessman.

TJ swallowed hard on the bile rising in her throat. With so many terrorist groups killing Americans, she found it hard to believe one of her own countrymen had done this terrible thing. The weight of the knowledge pressed down on her shoulders, slowing her feet until she came to a complete stop. She stared out over the canal, neither seeing the people on the other side, nor the rowers paddling canoes and kayaks along its smooth water.

All she could see was the glint of light in Sean's eyes as he bent to kiss her. She could still feel the touch of his hand on her bare skin, smoothing down her back and lower. For a man she'd only known two weeks, he'd left an indelible mark. A mark she'd fought hard to erase.

She turned and headed back to her apartment, continuing along the dirt towpath. She caught glimpses of people on the parallel paved path through the trees. One in particular sailed past her, his dark hair and tall build striking a chord of familiarity. Her heart leaped inside her chest and she had to talk herself down from the jolt.

Because she was thinking about Sean, had her mind superimposed his image on the man jogging the other trail? Despite reasoning, she picked up her pace to match that of the man's. Ahead, the two trails converged and she'd get a better view of him. Not that he was Sean. Sean died in Dindi. They'd taken him to the mortuary in the hospital's basement and shipped him out even before TJ could visit the body for confirmation. All the paperwork had been in order and his family had requested that his remains be shipped immediately.

After all the hoops the American government had gone through to get Congressman Haddock's body back to U.S. soil, TJ had questioned the speed with which Sean's body had left the hospital and country. At the time, she'd attributed it to the fact Haddock was a congressman, and everything in the government moved slower.

The trees and brush grew denser for several yards and TJ lost sight of the jogger. When she reached the trail convergence, blood pounded so hard against her eardrums she couldn't hear. A blond, athletic man emerged, not the dark-haired jogger she'd been racing to catch.

Feeling foolish, she slowed her breakneck pace, but she couldn't help scanning the side roads leading up to

K Street until she reached Rock Creek Parkway and headed north. Increasing her stride, she reached her street in less than fifteen minutes, cursing herself for allowing thoughts of Sean to manifest into a sighting.

After showering and slipping into work clothes, she pulled a bagel from the freezer and popped it into the toaster. Then she turned on the news, hoping the noise would fill her mind and block out the echoing sound of the explosion still ringing in her ears.

"WHERE HAVE YOU BEEN?" Kat Sikes stepped out of the conference room affectionately known as the War Room. In the ranks of the S.O.S. agents, shouting matches made it appear more like a war than a meeting of the minds. The good news was that everyone had a voice in the organization and no one was afraid to speak.

Still wearing the shorts and T-shirt from his morning jog, Sean had hoped to reach the locker room and shower on the fourth floor of the S.O.S. operations center without being waylaid. He stopped and faced Kat, his chest tightening at the dark circles beneath her eyes. "I was out jogging."

"Now don't look at me as though I'm going to fall apart." She reached up and cupped his chin. "I'm okay. Really."

"I worry about you."

"I know. But I'm doing much better." Kat smiled, although her lips were a little tight and her eyes were suspiciously bright. "Royce is looking for you." Before he could respond, she turned back to the conference room and shut the door behind her.

Sean sucked in a deep breath and let it out. How long

would it take to get over Marty's death? The man had
been his friend ever since they'd been in the military
together. Marty had been the one to introduce him to
Royce and the other S.O.S. agents, giving him a new
purpose in life since his discharge from the Army
Special Forces unit.

Marty married S.O.S. agent Kat Jenkins over a year ago
after a very stormy courtship and almost getting her killed
on a mission. Sean had stood beside Marty as his best man.

Forcing air past the tightness in his chest, Sean
reminded himself to breathe. A terrorist set off that
bomb at the embassy. A terrorist was responsible for
Marty's death.

If he'd been on time that day, he'd have died with
Marty, a situation he preferred over the gut-gnawing
guilt he harbored for his friend's death. He should have
died, too. Then he wouldn't have to see Kat's sad eyes
or listen to her sobs in the night. She'd moved into one
of the spare apartments in the upper level of the S.O.S.
building shortly after Marty's funeral. Right down the
hall from Sean's apartment.

He'd heard her crying when she thought no one was
around and he blamed himself every day since the
bombing for losing focus on the mission.

When he'd woken in the hospital late in the night,
he'd arranged for his body to be transferred to the
morgue, forging the paperwork indicating his own
"death" and resurfacing under another persona to
arrange for the immediate transfer of Marty's body back
to the States. It was the least he could do for his friend
when all he could wish for was to take Marty's place so
that Marty could be with his wife, alive and well.

He'd spent the next month hunting down leads on the terrorist responsible for the attack, pushing aside his longing for the woman he'd let get in the way of his duty. If he hadn't been with TJ that morning, he would have arrived on time. Maybe he'd have found the bomb or seen the terrorist coming or going from the embassy. Or perhaps he would have died in the explosion.

Since the attack, he'd made it his mission to discover who was behind the bombing and bring them down. Sean had already located Manu Attakora, a known terrorist-for-hire in Dindi. He'd found Manu's apartment with the terrorist dead inside, as if someone had been a step ahead of him in his search. Witnesses mentioned a dark-haired Anglo businessman seen coming and going from the apartment in the days prior to the bombing, but no one could give him a name.

Disappointed he didn't have the terrorist to question, Sean had located a laptop in Manu's apartment. He hoped it was the one Manu had used to communicate with the person who'd contracted him. Sean brought the computer back to the States and turned it over to S.O.S.'s resident computer guru. They hoped to have the files decrypted soon.

Back in the States, he'd done everything in his power to avoid running into a certain legislative assistant. His memories of TJ burned in his gut each day following the bombing. Damn it! He was an S.O.S. agent, not a fool in love.

Fools got killed or, through their actions or lack of actions, got others killed. As far as he was concerned, his involvement with TJ Barton was history and was not to be repeated.

Never mind that her face haunted his every memory and that the smell of springtime in D.C. reminded him of the scent of her hair. Today, jogging on the towpath along the C&O Canal, he felt her presence. She was here in D.C. and, even as large as the city was, with as many people working there daily, he stood a chance of seeing her again. A shorter haircut and sunglasses helped alter his appearance, but the woman wasn't dumb.

He chose to jog early in the morning to avoid any chance of running into her—or anyone else for that matter. Yet, even early in the morning, there were plenty of people getting their daily exercise. The beautiful weather brought out all manner of joggers, bicyclers and people out rowing.

He didn't know what he'd say if he ran into TJ. How would he explain to her his sudden "death" and reappearance? If the terrorists hadn't been aiming for Dindi's prime minister or Congressman Haddock and instead had wanted the S.O.S. team out of the way, he wanted to make sure they thought they'd accomplished the job.

As Sean passed through the office area, Casanova Valdez looked up from his terminal. "*Hola,* McNeal." He leaped to his feet and pulled Sean into a big bear hug. "Heard you were back." Valdez hugged him like he hugged everyone, with a lot of backslapping and exuberance. From a large Latin-American family, he wasn't embarrassed by blatant demonstrations of emotion. "It's good to see you in one piece."

Sean suffered through the embrace, putting distance between them as soon as Valdez let go.

"Hey, Sean." Nicole Steele's voice, as smooth as liquid chocolate, drew his attention. Her nickname in the agency was Tazer for a good reason. Her soft blond hair and blue-gray eyes had deceived more than one unsuspecting male. Known for her deadly self-defense techniques, Tazer could take down a man twice her size and he'd never know what hit him. Thank goodness she was loyal to the S.O.S. team.

Sean nodded a greeting.

"Sorry about Marty." She gave him a weak smile. "It's good to have you back."

Damn. He should have jogged earlier to avoid this kind of reception. He didn't want the ranks of the S.O.S. converging on him. Not yet.

"It's good to be back." Although he said the words, he didn't mean them. Maybe he'd stayed in Dindi so long to avoid just such a meeting with the rest of the S.O.S. team. The organization was small, consisting of one leader and less than twenty agents. Some were out on assignment. The others gathered around him.

The walls closed in on Sean. He needed air.

"Sean, glad you're back." Royce stepped out of his office. "I want to talk to you."

Glad for an escape, Sean eased through the team to stand in front of Royce. "That's what Kat said."

Royce motioned toward his office. "Why don't you come in and take a seat?"

Sean glanced down at his sweaty clothes and running shoes. "So long as you don't mind a little sweat."

"Not at all." He patted his tight abdomen. "Need to get out and exercise myself. I spend entirely too much time behind the desk."

Sean followed the older man into his office and dropped into a brown leather armchair.

Royce didn't have a spare ounce of flesh on his body. He was as tough and athletic as when he'd left the Navy SEALs ten years ago. "I know how personally you've taken Marty's death in Dindi, and I admit I'm concerned."

"Don't be. I'm going to find who killed him if it's the last thing I do."

"Yeah, but you might lose yourself in the process. You threw yourself into the investigation before you'd fully recovered, and you haven't taken any time off to decompress."

Sean frowned. He didn't like the way this conversation was going. "You can't take me off this case. I was there. I have to find who did this."

Royce raised a hand. "Relax. I won't take you off. But I want you to know I'm watching you. If you show any signs of cracking, I'll yank you off this case so fast you won't know what hit you. Agreed?"

"Agreed." Sean breathed in a deep breath and let it out. "Is that why you asked me in here?"

"No, intel came available you might be interested in."

"If it has anything to do with the bombing, you're right, I'm interested."

"Tim got past the encrypted password on the laptop you found in the terrorist's apartment. He found an enlightening e-mail on it."

"Anything about Manu's partner or who's behind the bombing?"

"No, but we did find Congressman Haddock's daily itinerary while in Dindi."

Sean stared down at his hands. That cleared the theory the bomber had gone after the S.O.S. agents.

"So the terrorist wasn't aiming for the Dindian prime minister or just any American."

"Right. They were targeting Haddock." Royce tapped the top of his desk with his index finger. "The interesting thing about the e-mail was that it originated from a staff member in Congressman Crane's office."

Sean pushed to his feet, hope leaping inside him. "You got a name?"

His boss nodded. "Yeah."

"Have you called him in for questioning?"

"Not quite."

"What do you mean?"

"The e-mail account is from one of the legislative assistants who accompanied Haddock to Dindi."

Sean immediately thought of TJ and just as quickly dispelled the thought. TJ worked for Haddock, not Crane. "Who was it?"

"George Fenton."

Recognizing the name, Sean shook his head. "Wasn't he—"

"One of the men who died in the bombing?" Royce nodded.

"Why would he set up a bombing that would take his own life? It doesn't make sense, unless he was playing a martyr."

"It was dated from the second day of Haddock's stay there and overlaps one of the meeting times Haddock had all his legislative assistants with him. We don't think George sent it. My bet is someone else sent it from back here in the States using George's log-on. I also got news from my contact in the CIA."

Sean dropped into a chair in front of Royce's desk

ready to absorb everything the man had to say. A burning sensation built in his chest and radiated outward.

"A lobbyist down on K Street has been pushing Congressman Crane to support the MC application of a different African nation than Dindi, one called Arobo."

"Arobo is contiguous to Dindi." Sean sat forward. "Damn."

"Yeah. It bears looking into."

"Haddock was on the verge of getting approval for the Millennium Challenge funding for Dindi. I heard that the congressman's death pretty much shut down the negotiations. In which case, Dindi won't be seeing any money from the United States."

"That's what I thought until I checked." Royce lifted a sheet of paper from his desk and passed it to Sean. "Not only is Dindi still being pushed, but Congresswoman Ann Malone is leading the effort."

Sean glanced at a copy of a fax without reading the print. "So does Haddock's death have anything to do with the MC funding or not?"

"Good question." Royce's eyes narrowed. "That's why I want you on the inside for this one."

"Inside where? With the lobbyist?"

"No. I signed you on as a staff assistant for Congresswoman Malone. She's in the office next to Crane. That should get you close. If Crane's push for Arobo has anything to do with the deaths in Dindi, you'll be there to find out and also to protect the congresswoman if need be."

Already feeling the necktie's stranglehold, Sean stretched the collar of his T-shirt. "You know TJ Barton works in that building. She'll recognize me."

"We'll have to take that risk. We can't afford not to."

Royce's lips twisted into a wry grin. "You're the charming type, I'm sure you'll think of something."

Sean wasn't so sure.

Royce leaned his elbows on his desk. "Do you want me to send Valdez or Tazer?"

An image of Marty dying in his arms surfaced. Sean's lips firmed into a straight line. "No. I want to find the bastard who did this."

"That's what I thought."

"We may have to bring TJ in on the mission to get her cooperation." Sean's gut tightened at the thought.

"Use your best judgment." Royce settled back in his chair and lifted the phone, the session ended, his mind already moving forward to other matters. "Dust off your best suits, McNeal. You're going to work in the Rayburn Building."

Chapter Three

TJ knocked on the open door and stepped into the spacious office lined with wood paneling and rich carpeting. "Congressman Crane, you're due at the White House in half an hour."

"That damned CIA's been crawling all over this office for the past three hours, asking me questions—and everyone else down to the new temp we just hired."

This was news. "Why?"

"It has something to do with the bombing in Dindi." Crane slammed his pen onto the desk. "Don't know why they picked me to target with questions. It isn't as if I had anything to do with the bombing. Just because I backed Arobo doesn't mean I'd kill to get the funding." He stood, slipped into his jacket and nodded at the papers in the middle of his desk. "I'll need a summary of these reports by the end of the day."

"Yes, sir." As Crane moved toward the door, TJ gathered the papers. A plain manila folder lay to the side of the others. "Do you want me to take this one, too?"

His hand paused in buttoning his jacket. "No, I'll handle that one myself." Crane brushed at his lapels and stood by the door waiting for her.

She shrugged and followed. Congressman Haddock had given her free rein of his office. Crane hadn't learned to trust her yet and from all accounts of other staff members who'd had the pleasure of working with him, he didn't allow anyone in his office when he wasn't there.

When TJ stepped past Crane, he turned to lock the door behind her, muttering, "They'll have to come back with a search warrant if they want in my office."

TJ stared after Crane until he disappeared. Then she glanced around the office where his staff scurried to straighten their desks.

So, the CIA had been here in Crane's offices? Why would they think Crane or someone in his office had anything to do with the bombing in Dindi? Her contact in the CIA had indicated an American had been at the root of the bombing. Could that American be someone in the Rayburn Building?

As she made her way back to her desk, goose bumps raised the fine hairs on her arms. Her office was still located in the same suite she'd shared with Haddock, but until a replacement was elected next month back in Texas, she'd be working for Crane. Which shouldn't have been a big deal. Both congressmen worked for the same political party and were on many of the same committees. TJ was familiar with most of the committee agendas and what was at stake.

TJ dodged people moving in and out of offices along the hallway. As she passed Congresswoman Ann Malone's office the door opened and Gordon Harris stepped out and turned back to say, "John, if you need anything, you have my cell number."

"Thanks, Gordon." The low baritone response sound-

ing from inside the office struck a note of familiarity
with TJ and she peered around Gordon to see the owner
of the voice.

Gordon turned toward her, pulling the door closed
behind him. "Oh, TJ, I'm glad you're here. I have some
documents I need you to take a look at and return to me
by tomorrow."

Just as the door closed, she caught a glimpse of the
man he'd been talking to. Her heart slammed to a halt
and the papers in her hands slipped to the floor.

"Whoa, let me help you with those." Gordon bent to
gather the sheets scattered over the floor. When he
stood, he frowned. "You all right? You look as if you'd
seen a ghost."

"I think I have." Suddenly light-headed, she took the
papers from Gordon without looking, her eyes on the
door as if willing it to open. "Wh-who was that you were
talking to?"

Gordon glanced back at the wood-paneled door as if
he could see through it. "You mean John? That's the new
temporary staff assistant for Congresswoman Malone.
Name's John Newman." He turned back to her, his eyes
narrowed. "Why? You know him?"

"No." The blood returned to her head in a rush. She'd
imagined Sean on the jogging trail and now she was hal-
lucinating at the office. What the hell was wrong with
her? Her face burned with embarrassment. "I have to go."

"What about those documents I need reviewed by
tomorrow?"

"Bring them by anytime, I'll look at them." *Just not
now.* She needed a few minutes alone to get a grip on
herself. She dashed to her office, dumped the stack of

papers on her desk and headed straight for the ladies restroom. When she reached an individual stall, she slid the bolt home and collapsed against the door.

Why, after a month had passed from the incident, was she having hallucinations? TJ shook her head. As if by shaking her head she could get her brain to return to normal!

Since the bombing, she'd had nightmares about the exploding building, about the hospital afterward and about Sean. She'd never had her bad dreams recur during the daylight hours. Were they taking over her life?

TJ rubbed at the stiff muscles in the back of her neck and stared at the glossy floor and wall tiles. A shaky laugh escaped her lips. Had the bombing in Dindi reduced her to hiding in a bathroom stall? Her shoulders straightened.

No. She was made of sterner stuff than that. After a few cleansing breaths, she opened the door, ready to face the world, her imaginings and herself.

She crossed to the sink and splashed water on her face. With a paper towel, she patted her cheeks dry and gazed at the stranger staring back at her from the mirror. Was that really her? Sure, she went through the motions every day of getting ready for work, but she hadn't stopped lately to take stock of her appearance. Since when had the dark circles appeared beneath her eyes and why did her cheeks look so sunken? Damn, she looked like walking death.

Just because Haddock and Sean had died in the explosion didn't mean she had to.

Get a grip, girl.

Less shaky and more in control of her emotions, TJ

pinched a little color into her cheeks and stepped out of the ladies restroom into the hall. She poured herself into her work, determined to be too busy to think by the end of the day, hoping that she'd fall into bed so tired, she'd sleep without the awful nightmares.

SEAN WORKED ALL DAY in Congresswoman Malone's office learning the ropes and the pecking order. Which was fine by him. The more they sent him to deliver documents, the more he got to see and hear.

Each time he worked his way down the hallway, he kept an eye open for TJ Barton. She'd mentioned working in the Rayburn Building and that Haddock had offices here. One half of him wanted to see her just to know where exactly she was. The other, more practical half knew meeting up with her again could blow his cover all to hell. An S.O.S. agent needed anonymity to do his job. The less she knew and the less he saw of her, the better.

On the pretext of making a good impression on the boss, Sean hung around the office late. He planned to stay until after everyone left so he could sneak into Congressman Crane's office.

After seven in the evening, Sean's assigned mentor, Gordon Harris, stopped by his desk and plucked a file out of the in-box. "Good, I was expecting this." Most of the staff had left by six. "Does the congresswoman have you loaded up with assignments already?"

"Not really. I'm reading all the material you gave me earlier and some available on the intranet to better understand what goes on around here."

Gordon shoved the file folder into his briefcase and

zipped the top. "Well don't stay too long. You'll absorb a lot of this over time."

He didn't have the luxury of time. "I know, but I want to come up to speed quickly. I hear Congresswoman Malone can be tough."

"She's demanding, but she knows her stuff. I wouldn't be surprised if she makes a bid for president some day."

While he had Gordon, he might as well question him. "I read somewhere that Malone is carrying the banner for the Dindi Millennium Challenge funding. I thought after the bombing, they'd cancel it."

"She's a powerhouse when it comes to backing a cause she believes in. The Appropriations Committee will vote on it in a few days. I'm betting my money on Malone."

The hairs on the back of Sean's neck stood at attention and he made a mental note to look up the Appropriations Committee's meeting schedule and location. "Is there any opposition?"

Gordon snorted. "Some." A diplomatically vague answer to be expected from a legislative assistant.

Sean had overheard rumblings that Congressman Crane was foaming at the mouth because Dindi didn't get dropped when Haddock died. He'd backed Arobo all along. It would be interesting to see the outcome. Malone and Crane were both from the same party and on the same committee, and they couldn't agree. But was that reason enough to have Haddock killed? Sean's mind ticked through the possibilities. Could the members be playing political games gone deadly? "How long have you worked with Malone?"

"Since she was elected six years ago." Gordon glanced at his watch. "I've got to get out of here. I'm supposed to meet a friend for dinner and I'm already late. You need anything before I go?"

"No, I'll only be another thirty minutes before I cut out."

"See ya tomorrow."

After Gordon left, Sean remained in his seat and pulled up the internal roster of congressmen and staff members. Crane had a staff of twenty-one full-timers and four temps; apparently he hadn't replaced George Fenton. Malone had a staff of twenty-two and four temps, counting him. How many people would they have to cross-reference with the CIA background checks before they got to the right one? He printed a copy of the staff lists to give to Royce. His first stop in Crane's office had to be George's desk. He glanced at the time. Eight o'clock. Still early for snooping in another congressman's office. Instead, he spent time going through all the desks and drawers of the staff members in Malone's office, saving her inner sanctum for last.

Before he tackled the congresswoman's office, he made a pass through the suite and poked his head out into the hallway. No one moved and, other than a few lights shining beneath doorways farther down the hallway, he didn't see anyone. Then a door down the hall opened.

Sean ducked back in and listened for footsteps. They headed in the opposite direction.

Good. If he hurried, he could get into Malone's office and close the door before anyone saw him. Sean hurried back to the congresswoman's office, slipping a thin plastic lock pick from his pocket.

TIRED AND READY to call it a day, TJ left her office with a stack of inner-office mail envelopes marked with suspense dates of tomorrow. After she dropped these at various offices along the corridor, she could go home and heat up the leftover Chinese food she had in her refrigerator. Then again, would it be any good after four days?

She dropped two envelopes in Congressman Latke's office and turned back to hit Crane and Malone's offices.

Maybe just a piece of toast and a long soak in a hot bath.

Her plans made, TJ entered Malone's office. Her feet sank into the plush carpeting, muffling the sound of her footfalls as she passed through the suite to get to Gordon's desk positioned outside Malone's door.

As she neared the inner-office area, a clicking sound alerted her that she wasn't alone. Was Gordon still here? If so, she could explain her comments on the report she'd reviewed.

Rounding the corner to Gordon's office, her mouth open to say hello, TJ stopped and stared at the empty room. Should she add hearing things to her list of hallucinations? Pressing her ear to Malone's door, she listened for any signs of a late meeting with the congresswoman. No sounds penetrated the wooden door to the office.

The hairs on the back of TJ's neck rose to attention and she had the uncanny sense of being watched. With more haste than care, she tossed the envelopes into Gordon's in-box and turned to leave, a chill snaking its way down her spine. She took a step and stopped. Was that the sound of a door? The one leading to the hallway? "Hello? Is anyone in here?" No one answered.

A distinct click sounded from the outer office area. Had she left the door open and it had swung closed behind her? Her breath caught in her throat as she made her way back through the offices to the hallway. The door that she'd left open a moment before was now closed.

Creepy. TJ jerked the door open and stepped out into the hallway and breathed a sigh, chastising herself for letting her imagination get the better of her.

Then she saw him.

A man hurried down the hallway toward the exit.

What the hell? Had he been in Malone's office snooping around? Should she call the Capitol Police and have him stopped? What if she was wrong and the man was rushing to meet his family for dinner?

TJ's feet moved in the direction the man had gone. Maybe she'd follow him just to see who it was. What could that hurt? If he had been snooping, at least she might be able to give more of a description than the back of a man's shadowy head.

The man disappeared around a corner.

Now, she could run and he wouldn't know she was chasing after him. TJ slipped out of her shoes, clutched them in her hands and ran down the hall as fast as she could in her confining skirt and bare feet. When she neared the corner, she slowed and peered around.

The man had disappeared. How could she describe him if she didn't actually see his face? If she didn't hurry, he'd make the parking garage and escape before she had a chance to identify him.

Why she should be so fixated, she didn't stop to question. Perhaps her earlier Sean "sightings" were making her punchy. Determined to catch up to the un-identified man, she hitched up her skirt and lit out at a jog, rounding the next corner at a flat-out run.

A hand reached out and snagged her arm, jerking her

back against a solid wall of muscle. Another hand clamped over her mouth, muffling the scream rising in her throat. Her shoes slipped from her hands, dropping to the floor.

Instinct kicked in and she bit the hand, stomped on the man's instep and cocked her elbow to jab into his gut.

At that moment, a voice penetrated her fog of panic.

"Damn it. Stop fighting me and I'll let you go." That voice. The same voice she'd heard earlier today coming out of Malone's office. Her body froze, her skin tingling all over.

The hand over her mouth loosened. "Are you going to scream?"

TJ shook her head. She couldn't scream if all the air had left her lungs. Hell, she couldn't breathe.

He dropped his hand and slowly turned her to face him. "Why were you chasing me?"

All the blood drained from TJ's face and the man's image swam in her vision like an apparition floating through a cloud. When her knees buckled, she staggered backward until her back hit the wall. "Sean?"

Chapter Four

Sean gripped TJ's arms to keep her from falling. Her face blanched and her eyes widened. Her knees shook as if she was about to drop to the floor in a dead faint, or so he told himself as he pulled her against his chest.

The scent of spring flowers wafted beneath his nose, sending him back to Dindi and the hotel suite he'd shared with this beautiful woman. For a long moment he allowed the good memories to wash over him. He wanted to continue holding her close until he recaptured that feeling of belonging he'd only experienced with her in that faraway room. But the good feelings were chased away by bad memories. The blinding flash of the explosion and the resulting blackness filled his mind.

Marty was dead. Sean had only sustained minor injuries—cuts, scrapes, ruptured eardrums and a mild concussion. He'd survived. Marty hadn't.

With cold determination, he set TJ at arm's length and stepped away. Somehow, he had to get through this mission without letting this woman distract him again. Detecting movement to his left, he painted a confused but friendly expression on his face. "Why were you following me? Do I know you?" He bent to retrieve her shoes and handed them to her.

As she slipped them on, her skin went from white to red in a manner of seconds. "Do I—"

The night-duty Capitol Police guard chose that moment to walk by. "Good evening, Ms. Barton." The guard gave Sean a wary look. "Everything okay here?"

TJ pushed a hand through her shoulder-length hair and gave a shaky laugh. "Oh, hi, Joe. Yes, yes, of course." When the guard turned away from her, TJ glared at Sean.

"If you're sure…" Joe didn't act as if he wanted to leave.

"No, really, Joe," TJ said. "We were just discussing work, weren't we?"

Sean nodded, gauging TJ's words and anticipating her next with some trepidation. "Yes, sir."

"You new around here?" Joe asked.

"Started today in Congresswoman Malone's office." Sean stuck out his hand. "John Newman."

A soft snort sounded beside him.

As the guard took his extended hand, Sean could feel the heat of TJ's glare burning into his back. She could blow his cover if she wanted and she was mad enough to do it. He hoped she wouldn't.

"John Newman," the guard repeated. "Nice to meet you." He glanced again at TJ. "If you're sure you're okay, I'll be on my way. Still have my rounds to complete."

"I'm perfectly fine." Her brows rose. "And so is Se— John. He's perfectly fine." Her lips thinned for a moment before she graced the guard with a dazzling, albeit fake, smile. "Thanks for your concern. It's nice to know some people still care."

Joe walked away, glancing back once before he rounded the corner.

TJ clamped her mouth shut and crossed her arms over her chest, watching Sean until the guard's footsteps receded.

Sean didn't like pretending with TJ, but he had to maintain his cover. He'd practiced the lies he'd tell her half a dozen times, knowing it was only a matter of time before she discovered he was there.

After the policeman moved on, TJ grabbed Sean's arm and ushered him, none too gently, down the long hallway back to her empty office.

Sean assumed a casual, natural look in case someone was watching. Surely legislative assistants dragged the new guys down the halls at some point during the day. He didn't want to cause a scene or draw attention. His job was to blend in.

When she shoved him into her office and slammed the door behind him, her cheeks blazed with twin flags of color. She paced across the room and turned to face him. "I want answers and I want them now."

He took a deep breath, wondering how much to tell her. "I'm sorry I didn't acknowledge you in the hallway. I didn't want to draw a lot of attention."

"From whom? The place is practically deserted." She raised her eyebrows, her toe tapping on the floor. "Who are you really? Sean McNeal or John Newman?"

The story he'd concocted froze on his lips. He'd never had trouble lying to maintain his cover, until he'd met TJ. He swallowed hard and forced the lie out. "John Newman."

"And who is Sean McNeal? Just a name you made up to get me in bed in Dindi?"

He hated doing it, but he'd rather look the bastard than blow his cover and place himself, and possibly her, in danger. "That's right. I didn't want any complications after I left Dindi."

"Complications." For a moment her face paled again, then darkened into a ruddy red. A muscle ticked in her jaw for several long seconds. Then she shook her head. "I'm not buying it. Tell me what you're really up to or I'll call Joe back here and have you arrested."

Not sure whether or not she was bluffing, Sean's eyes narrowed. "On what charges?"

"Spying." Her own eyes widened and a gasp escaped her lips. "For all I know, you could have been the one to bomb the embassy."

Sean had known she wouldn't take his reappearance well, but this encounter wasn't going the way he'd rehearsed. If he didn't level with her, she could blow his cover. Question was: could he trust her? He stared long and hard at her. Hell, he'd have to. "TJ, I'm working undercover."

Her eyes narrowed. "What do you mean? Are you with the CIA or something?"

"Something like that. I can't tell you everything, but I need everyone to think I'm just staff assistant John Newman."

"Are you working the Dindi case?"

"Yeah." He closed the distance between them and

lifted her hands in his. "Look, I know this is hard to understand—"

"You have no idea." She jerked her hands free and crossed her arms over her chest. "One minute I'm making love to a man I thought I knew. The next, I'm told he died in an explosion."

"I'm sorry you had to go through that."

"Why should I believe you, now? How do I know *you* didn't orchestrate that explosion? Give me one good reason I shouldn't turn you into the police or FBI?"

Sean's arms crossed over his chest. "If that's what you think you need to do, go ahead."

Her wide eyes narrowed, but she didn't move for the phone. "Damn you! I don't know what to believe."

"I can't tell you any more than I'm undercover and need you to keep quiet."

When he reached out again, she backed away. "Don't touch me."

What did he expect? He'd left her alone in a foreign country thinking he was dead. After being away from her for a month, did he think she'd be happy to see him?

The spark in her eyes faded and the starch went out of her stance. "Tell me this. Were you working a case in Dindi?"

"Yes." His response revealed none of the emotion he felt, none of the regret, none of the memories. He couldn't afford to let them show.

Her eyes swam with tears and she whispered, "Was that all it was to you?"

Here's the part where he could say she meant more to him than just the case. The part where he could say he'd fallen for her and had begun to think of a more permanent relationship. The tears welling in her eyes almost had him spilling his feelings like a rookie.

Remember Marty. The silence stretched one, two, three seconds before he responded. "Yes, I was working a case." Better let her think he was a bastard. It made things easier.

She sucked in a breath and held it before she let it out slowly. "Thank you. At least I know exactly where we stand."

Where did they stand? Sean had a good idea, and it didn't involve happily-ever-after.

"You say you weren't responsible for the bombing in Dindi." She pinched the bridge of her nose, then her hand dropped to her side, her gaze leveling on him. "Why should I trust you? You've lied to me from the start, even faked your own death. You still haven't given me a good reason not to turn you in."

Sean welcomed her anger, the color rising in her cheeks and the fire in her eyes. He could handle it better than her tears. "I'm here to find out who's behind the bombing in Dindi."

"Here? Why didn't you find the terrorist in Dindi?"

"I found one of them and what I found there led me back here."

TJ sucked in a breath. "Here? In the Rayburn Building?" Her head moved from side to side.

"That's what it looks like." He stepped forward and reached for her hands, catching himself before he actually touched her. His hands fell to his sides. "We need to find all those responsible."

"I lost my boss and a couple of friends in that bombing." She looked as if she was going to add to that, but she clamped her lips shut and wrapped her arms around her midsection.

"I lost a good friend." Sean shoved a hand through his hair and stared at her. "That's why I'm here."

Her brow knitted in a frown. "You think someone in the Rayburn Building was responsible? A member or staffer?"

"Maybe. That's what I hope to find out."

"That would explain why the CIA were crawling all over Crane's office earlier today."

Sean nodded.

TJ's eyes narrowed again. "And in the meantime, I don't suppose you plan to keep me in the picture? No updates on your progress?"

He shook his head. "Knowing too much and snooping around could be dangerous."

"Bull. Like Dindi wasn't dangerous?"

"No kidding, TJ. Whoever funded that could be here and, who knows, might plan another incident."

"And you want me to just stand by and watch it happen?" She rolled her eyes. "Yeah, right."

He stared down into her eyes. "TJ, I need you to stay out of it. Don't ask questions." He didn't have time to monitor her efforts. He had to remain focused on the goal.

"How do you plan on finding this person? You don't even know anyone here."

"For starters, I need you to play dumb about knowing me."

"I don't have to play dumb. I never knew you."

That hurt, but Sean pushed on. "Do I have your promise to keep my identity to yourself?"

She hesitated. "I don't feel right about it. You could be the bad guy."

"Do you really think that?" He reached out and captured her hands, drawing her closer. "Do you really think I could bomb an embassy?" Staring down into her face, he could have fallen into those liquid brown eyes and forgotten what he was all about. But he needed her promise.

She didn't meet his eyes, her gaze falling short to somewhere around his mouth. Her tongue darted out and slid across her bottom lip. "I don't know."

"Trust me, TJ," he whispered, his mouth drawn to hers. When his lips claimed hers, he forgot his original question, forgot why he was here. All thought focused on kissing TJ Barton as though yesterday and tomorrow didn't exist.

Pulling back cost him, but eventually he did. "Do I have your promise?"

Brown eyes gazed up at him, glazed and unfocused. Then she stepped out of his arms and ran her hands over her skirt; bright spots of red highlighted her cheekbones. "I'll keep your secret for now. But, if I find you doing anything funny, I'll sic every cop in the Capitol complex on your butt."

"Define funny."

"Wiring the place for bombs, holding anyone hostage, you know, the usual terrorist activities."

He held up his hand. "I promise, no funny stuff."

"And one other thing…"

This one was going to be big if her pause was any indication. Sean breathed in, then out. "Okay, shoot."

"Promise me you won't kiss me again."

AFTER SEAN LEFT, TJ collapsed in the chair behind her desk and stared at the closed door.

What the hell? Her head spun and her gut ached as if she'd been sucker punched. Sucker was the word for it. She'd spent the last four weeks mourning the death of a man who never died. Had she really fallen in love with a man she'd known only two weeks? A man she hadn't known at all?

If only she'd known he hadn't died.

While she'd tossed, turned and barely slept from the nightmares, the louse had been alive. She smacked her palm on the desktop.

"Should I come back later?" Gordon Harris stood in the doorway, his brows high on his forehead.

TJ had been so deep in her thoughts, she hadn't heard the door open. "No, no, come in." She waved him in. She'd be damned if Sean McNeal got another minute of her thoughts. "What are you doing here so late?"

"I should ask you the same question." He dug in his briefcase and pulled out a stack of papers. "I forgot to leave the Budget Committee report and Representative Crane's changes to the speech for the Daughters of the American Revolution. Had to cut my dinner short when Malone called to remind me." He hesitated. "But if you'd rather wait, I could come back tomorrow when you don't look like you're going to bite my head off."

"I won't bite your head off. Let me see those." She held out her hand, her fingers wiggling impatiently.

"Okay, okay. Give me a second to get organized." As Gordon riffled through the stack of papers, Sean walked by the door behind him.

The way her pulse quickened brought back memories

of the first time she'd met Sean when she'd been scouting Conbanau prior to Congressman Haddock's visit.

Oh, how gullible she'd been. Was that what she was now?

So much for not giving the man another moment of her thoughts. He was in the same building. She couldn't ignore him. Hell, she felt compelled to keep an eye on him to make sure she wasn't harboring a criminal.

Gordon followed her gaze, turning to see what she was staring at.

He laid the papers in her in-box and straightened. "What's up with you?"

Her brain wasn't engaged in Gordon's words and she shook her head to clear her thoughts. "Huh?"

"I said, what's up with you?"

"Nothing." *A ghost just came to life and I'm supposed to pretend he didn't. Other than that, nothing.* What bothered her more was that kiss. If only he hadn't kissed her. Her lips still tingled from the contact. That spark was still there, damn it! He was a liar and a fake. She shouldn't have any other feelings than contempt for the man calling himself John Newman. Anger boiled within. Not so much at Sean, but at herself for falling right back into his charade.

"Are you still hurting over the guy that died in the bombing? Let me take you to dinner and we can talk about it."

The blond-haired, blue-eyed, boy-next-door good looks appealed to every other intern or single staffer on the floor. But not TJ. Unfortunately, she leaned toward black hair and green eyes. And she didn't have time to lean. A killer possibly lurked in the halls of the Rayburn Building.

Scarier still, the killer could be Sean McNeal, aka John Newman. She should be searching for clues. "You know how I feel about dating coworkers, Gordon." In the meantime, she had to pretend to live her life as an ordinary legislative assistant. She laid a hand over his and softened her expression. "The offer is tempting, but…no."

Gordon's brows drew together and he covered her hand. "You can't give up on all men just because of one, TJ."

"Who said I was giving up?" Slipping her hands free, she pushed her chair away from her desk and stood, moving to the far corner of the room, out of reach. "Gordon, did you ever think the Dindi bombing might have been someone other than a terrorist?"

He leaned against her desk and crossed his arms over his chest. "Why do you ask?"

Sean's words had been worrying her. That, on top of the information her CIA connections had unearthed. Could that American be in this building? "Just for the sake of conjecture, what if someone wanted it to look like a terrorist job? Who would want Congressman Haddock dead and why?"

Gordon blew out a stream of air. "Wow, I hadn't thought of that."

"Surely, Haddock had enemies," she pressed.

Gordon shrugged. "Every representative has their share of dissatisfied constituents and competitors."

"Why would someone want Haddock dead though?"

"Could be a number of reasons."

TJ leaned against the wall. "Name some."

"His pro-choice views on abortion for one. There's always someone willing to bomb an abortion clinic. I guess they could target a congressman against the pro-life movement."

"Maybe. But why bomb an embassy in a foreign country when they blow up abortion clinics in the States? What else?"

"If it were an election year, I'd say a worried opponent facing a loss at the polls. But the election's not for another thirteen months."

"No, election year isn't right." TJ paced the length of the office and back. "What about the committees he's on? Is there anyone vehemently opposed to his decisions?"

"No more than usual." Gordon rubbed his chin and stared at the ceiling in the far corner of the office. "He was in Africa working on securing the Millennium Challenge funding for the Dindi government. Maybe someone didn't want him to get that funding." His gaze moved to hers. "You think someone around here had it in for Haddock? If it was the MC funding, they could go after Malone. She's backing Dindi like Haddock did."

"No, I'm sure it's nothing. No use getting Malone all worried." TJ didn't want to alarm Gordon or anyone else in the building because she'd had a wild thought and a small piece of unsubstantiated evidence. "I keep thinking about when that building exploded. It's still all a blur to me. I was outside the building when the bomb went off. What if I saw something that could help identify the killer?"

Gordon's brows rose high on his forehead. "Did you see something?"

"Not that I can remember. That's just it. From the moment I stepped on the embassy grounds to the time I woke in the hospital is all a big black hole."

"Have you thought about a hypnotist?" Gordon's eyes narrowed and he stared hard at her. "You should try that."

She shrugged. "It's probably nothing. Besides, it's been a month."

"Then why'd you bring it up?"

"I keep having dreams about it. The whole thing replays in my head and I feel like I'm missing something." At least Gordon had given her some ideas to pursue. TJ stood. "I left some documents with one of Crane's legislative assistants. I need to collect them before I head home."

"What about the report and the speech?"

"Leave them here on my desk. I'm not done for the night. Thanks for listening." TJ stepped into the hallway and almost ran into Congresswoman Malone and Congressman Crane.

The congresswoman was dressed in a simple black cocktail dress. Crane wore the same suit he'd had on earlier that day.

"Oh there you are, Gordon. Glad you could come back in on such short notice." Malone nodded briefly at TJ. "Are you headed home, Ms. Barton?"

"In a little while. It's been a long night." TJ smiled at Congressman Crane. "Do you need anything before I leave?"

"No, thank you. I'm just collecting a report from my office before I head home myself."

"Then you two have a good evening." Malone moved down the hallway dictating a list of tasks for Gordon to accomplish.

Did the woman never know when to quit? She often worked Gordon late into the evenings. Haddock had had his occasional late night, but not as often as Malone.

Crane's gaze followed Malone and Gordon. "Couldn't help overhearing your conversation with Harris. You still thinking about the bombing?"

TJ nodded and fell in step with the congressman, entering his suite of offices. "The dreams haven't gone away. I keep thinking I could have seen someone and I can't make the memory surface."

"You could be suffering post-traumatic stress syndrome. Have you considered seeing a psychiatrist?"

"Not yet." Between Crane and Gordon, they'd have her going to every shrink in D.C. for her "problem."

"Don't wait until you can't think straight." He unlocked his office door. "Have a good evening."

"Good night, sir." TJ collected her documents and walked away shaking her head. Crane giving her advice wasn't something she'd expected out of this evening.

Thirty minutes later, she climbed into her compact car and drove out of the parking garage. On the short drive to her apartment, she had all the quiet she could stand with thoughts of Sean resurfacing at every corner.

Who would have wanted Congressman Haddock dead and why? If they wanted to stop the Millennium Challenge funding, the bombing hadn't accomplished that. Congresswoman Ann Malone had taken up the fight to get that money approved. Sean hadn't said anything about other attempts, but could Malone be next?

As TJ slowed to round a corner leading to her street, she noticed another set of headlights behind her on the deserted street. Hadn't she seen those same headlights for the past two turns she'd made on her way home?

She drove past her apartment complex and turned down another road, just to be sure.

Two blocks sped by and the headlights appeared in her rearview mirror.

TJ's stomach clenched. Someone was following her. Could it be Sean? Did she want to stop and ask? Hell no.

Pressing her foot to the accelerator, she raced to the next street and turned left without slowing or signaling. Once around the corner, she searched for a side street and darted down one with cars parked along the side. Cutting her headlights, she downshifted to slow her car without using the breaks, sliding into a spot behind another car against the curb. Before the headlights appeared, she'd killed the engine.

She ducked low in her seat and waited. Less than a minute went by and the headlights moved slowly along the other street, passing the one she'd turned on.

Even after the car passed, TJ remained where she was, her heart pounding in her ears. How long should she wait? Was she being paranoid?

Headlights appeared at the end of the street in front of her and TJ's heart skipped a beat. Crud. Maybe she wasn't just paranoid. Maybe someone was following her.

TJ sank lower in her seat as the car drifted by. Unable to see over the top of the dash or the side of the door, she held her breath as the sound of an automobile engine passed. It did pass, and shortly after, TJ eased her head up. The car was gone and the street was empty of any oncoming traffic.

Turning the key in the ignition, TJ almost had a heart attack when the little car wouldn't start. On a second twist of the key, the engine sprang to life. The rest of her trip to her apartment remained blessedly uneventful.

Outside her apartment door, her hands shook as she jammed the key into the lock. She'd glanced over her shoulder at least ten times before her apartment door opened, expecting the eerie headlights to reappear on the street or a bogeyman to jump out of the bushes at any minute.

Once inside, she slammed her door shut and slid the bolt home. That wasn't enough. A quick trip through the two bedrooms, kitchen and living space finally set her mind at ease. No one had come into her apartment while she'd been at work. A quick glance out the darkened windows confirmed no one lurked in the street.

A shaky laugh escaped her and she collapsed onto the couch, dropping her head into her hands. Sean's reappearance had shaken her more than she cared to admit.

She forced a laugh, then almost choked on it when headlights shone through the filmy curtains of her living-room window. A car cruised by on her street like a snake sliding through the grass in search of its next meal.

Chapter Five

"Learning anything?" Royce stopped by Sean's desk shortly after midnight.

"Don't you ever go home?" Sean asked.

"Since home is upstairs, I'm always at home."

"Let me rephrase. Don't you ever leave the office?"

Royce shrugged. "Slow television night." Sean knew Royce used to have a family. A wife and a son. The wife died in an auto accident and the son disappeared his second year at Georgetown University. With no one expecting him, he didn't really have a home to go to.

Sean understood not having a home or someone awaiting his return. For a short time he'd dreamed of TJ filling that role.

"Anyone else working?" Royce glanced over the tops of the cubicles the agents used when they worked in the office. Mostly, they operated in the field.

"The last time I checked, Tim was back in his corner hacking away at the bank account the CIA traced to the terrorist in Dindi."

"Any leads?"

"Not yet." So far, Tim hadn't been able to get past the

bank's firewall. Even when they did break in, the chances of the account pointing to an individual were slim, which meant additional digging into shell corporations.

"What about the legislative assistant who was with Haddock in Dindi, TJ Barton? Have you run into her? Any chance of getting close to her?"

Sean stiffened. At one time they'd been close. But that wasn't what Royce meant. "Yes, I've run into her. She's in Haddock's old office, two doors down from mine." He hadn't told Royce anything about his previous life with TJ.

"Did she recognize you?"

"Yes. I had to tell her I was working undercover."

"Couldn't lie your way out of it?"

Sean shook his head. "No, she's former FBI and too smart for the lies." He hadn't told Royce why TJ had been the only one of her party who'd escaped injury.

"You look like a man with a lot on his mind." Royce dropped into the chair beside Sean's desk. "If it has anything to do with this case, spill it."

Royce gave him the opening. Why did he find it so difficult to talk about what happened between him and TJ? He'd misplaced his focus in Dindi, he didn't want to risk losing this assignment because Royce lost faith in his objectivity. Honesty won out. "There's something you ought to know about what happened in Dindi."

"You mean more than what you've already told me?"

"Yeah." He hesitated. How did he tell Royce he'd fallen for a stranger in less than two weeks? Hell, in less than two hours. He'd traveled all over the world with the Army Special Forces and then again with S.O.S. And in a small country in Africa, he'd found TJ. What were the odds?

"Is this about the affair you had with Haddock's assistant?" Royce asked.

Sean's gaze snapped to Royce. "How did you know?"

A sad smile tipped the corners of the older man's mouth. "Marty told me about her the morning he died." Royce's lips tightened into a thin line. "He was glad to see you falling hard after all the ribbing you gave him about marrying Kat."

Sean nodded, remembering. "I did give him hell. Felt like I was losing my best friend."

Royce stared at a snapshot hanging on the wall of Sean, Marty and Kat on mountain bikes in the North Carolina hills. "You didn't lose a brother in Marty, you gained a sister in Kat."

"I did lose him in the end."

"And you're blaming your relationship with the Barton woman on it, aren't you?"

Sean pounded his fist on the desk. "Yes." He rolled back from his desk and stood. "If I hadn't been playing around—"

"You'd be dead, too." Royce stood. "Not only would Kat have lost her husband, she'd have lost her friend. You've been the only one keeping her from falling apart. None of us are as close to her as you are. She needs you. Face it. You weren't meant to die." Royce laid a hand on his shoulder. "It wasn't your time."

"And it was Marty's?" He shook loose of Royce's hand, anger burning a hole in his gut.

"Yes, damn it." Royce crossed his arms over his chest. "Don't get me wrong, I cared for Marty as much as anyone, and I never wished bad things to happen, but his number was up." With his feet braced apart and his eyes blazing, Royce had only just begun his tirade. "You didn't die in that attack for a reason. And that reason was to find out what really happened. Are you going to pull your head out of feeling sorry for yourself long enough to accomplish your mission? Or do I need to find a replacement with a better perspective?"

Hands clenched into fists. Sean wanted to strike out, hit someone. The anger he'd fed off for the past month boiled up and threatened to overflow into action. Royce's words struck him like a blow and he wanted to hit back. But Royce Fontaine was his friend, not the enemy. Not the person responsible for the deaths of Congressman Haddock, Marty Sikes and many others. Someone else had ordered that attack.

"Are you on the case?" Royce asked.

Sean straightened his shoulders, drawing on his years of military service and ability to work under extreme pressure. "I'm on."

"Then stop beating yourself up."

Sean's jaw clenched. "Is that an order, boss?"

"Damn right. And get in tight with Barton. She might be able to get into places you won't have access to as temporary staff."

He should have seen it coming, but Royce was a pro at manipulating the best of them. Sean hated that he'd been gullible enough to fall for Royce's technique. "Sneaky bastard."

Royce's brows rose. "We do whatever it takes."

Meaning Sean had to get in with TJ or any other staff member in order to determine who the hell backed that bombing. "Okay, I'll work with TJ." But he would not fall for her again or lose his perspective.

Sean's boss gave him a slap on the back. "Thought you'd see it my way."

Royce may think he had it all sewn up, but Sean knew TJ Barton wasn't a pushover. She might see things in an entirely different light. So much for keeping his distance from the one woman who could blow his cover. "I hope she sees it your way, too."

"That's where you turn on the McNeal charm."

It would take a lot more than charm to get under TJ Barton's defenses after Dindi.

A whoop went up from the computer lab.

Royce turned and stepped out into the hallway. "Let's go see what Tim found."

At EIGHT O'CLOCK the following morning, TJ had already been at work for two hours. Just because they'd lost Congressman Haddock didn't mean the work went away. He hadn't been the only official lost in the bombing. They'd also lost Bryce Chumley, the legislative director, and Monique Tyler, Haddock's executive assistant. Additional duties of their lost comrades were divvied out to the remaining already overloaded staff. The projects everyone had been working transferred to other congressmen within the party for oversight.

So, why waste time pretending to sleep when there was more work to be done than this one legislative assistant could accomplish? With testimonies to read, reports to write and condense, documents to file and recommendations to make, sleep became a highly overrated commodity.

Who was she trying to kid? She hadn't slept all night because every time she closed her eyes, she saw headlights beaming in her rearview mirror. If not the head-lights, Sean McNeal stared at her from the pile of rubble standing where the American embassy had been. She thought she'd had nightmares before Sean rose from the dead. His revelation about the bombing possibly origi-nating from the Rayburn Building had her alternating between scared and angry all night long.

The carpet next to her bed lay flat with the amount of pacing she'd done into the wee hours. And the more she paced, the madder she steamed. Her anger stemmed from the so-called American who had killed other Americans. She also couldn't deny her anger at Sean McNeal for letting her mourn his death when all along he'd been alive and well. If Sean had stepped into her apartment last night, she couldn't have been held re-sponsible for her actions.

The secret inner part of her finally won out and rejoiced that he hadn't in fact died. After all the grief, her heart lightened for the first time in the weeks since her return. But that didn't excuse him for leading her to believe he was dead. She still wanted to give back a little of the anguish he'd caused her. Her anger spiked higher when she considered revenge on a live Sean McNeal when she should be more concerned about a killer running loose in the halls of the Rayburn Building.

Who could it be?

A knock sounded at her door and TJ's heart thudded against her chest. Instead of wading through the stacks of documents awaiting her attention, she'd been review-ing her own list of possible suspects and wondering which ones Sean had already checked out.

Had her thoughts of Sean conjured him from her

wild imaginings? She shook her head and called out, "The door's open."

The door filled with the man foremost in her thoughts and nightmares. With his short dark hair neatly combed back from his face and wearing a charcoal suit and red tie, Sean could have stepped off the cover of a fashion magazine and melted any female heart he set his sights on. "Hey, TJ."

Air left her lungs in a whoosh and she spun her chair away, pressing her hands into her lap to keep them from shaking. He had no right to look that cool, calm and collected when she teetered on the edge of exploding. Panic raced through her, shutting down her brain's capacity to reason.

The door clicked behind her and Sean's low rumbling voice spoke softly. "We need to talk."

"What more is there to say? You lied, you died, and I fell for it. I'm not gullible enough to fall a second time. End of story. Now go away." TJ attributed her accelerated heartbeat to anger. Not because Sean's voice and the scent of his aftershave brought back all the memories and feelings she'd had for him back in Dindi. Damn him for living and damn him for cutting her out of this investigation.

"TJ, I have some information about the bombing. I thought you'd be interested." He paused, then added, "But if you're not, I won't bother you."

The carrot dangled in front of her. As hard as she tried to resist, she couldn't. She had to know what he'd found. She sighed and swiveled her chair to face him, suspicion drawing her brows together. "I thought you didn't want me involved."

"I changed my mind." He shook his head. "No, I was wrong. Having an ally on the inside could help me sort things out faster."

He was good at this. The man almost sounded sincere. "I have a job to do."

"You have a country to save."

TJ closed her eyes. Sean McNeal knew how to play her all along. "Don't get all patriotic on me. You want something and you'll manipulate me to get it. What is it you want?"

"Your cooperation in this investigation."

"You already have my promise not to reveal your true identity." She laughed. "Although what that is, I haven't a clue."

"Look, I'm willing to share a little information in exchange for your assistance." As he spoke, he crossed the room until he towered over her desk. "Are you interested in what our computer tech found, or are you going to argue? I don't have time to argue."

TJ sat back in her chair, impressed by his seriousness and determination, not to mention the intimidation factor of having a hulking man breathing fire over her. Intimidation always riled her. "I'm interested."

"Good." For a moment, he stood stiff and unbending, glaring down at her from his six-foot-three-inch frame. "Our computer tech traced money transferred back to an account in the Caribbean Islands. After a little more digging, he linked the account to a corporation here in the metro area. We have an address." He held up a computer printout of a city map and directions. "I'm going to pay them a visit this morning."

From a man who didn't want her to know anything,

he sure was in a sharing mood. Should she trust him? TJ hesitated. He'd lied to her once, why wouldn't he lie to her again? "Why are you telling me all this?"

"If I keep you informed, you might help me in other ways."

Ah, the trade-off. She wasn't sure she liked his vague comment. Was he only using her again? "Other ways? For instance?"

"I'll let you know when I need the favor returned."

Her back teeth ground together. "Your idea smells."

Sean crossed his arms over his chest and stood straight. "Take it or leave it."

She had the chance to find out more information that could lead to the discovery of who bombed the embassy. Should she trust him enough to be on the up and up? *Hell, no.* Did she want to find the person responsible for the bombing? *Hell, yeah.* However, she didn't want Sean to think she was falling for his dangled carrot so easily. "What about Congress-woman Malone or her chief of staff? Won't they wonder where you are?"

"I've told them I still have some in-processing to complete. They bought it. Besides, Malone has an Appropriations Committee meeting today."

She closed the file she'd been staring at and stood. "I'm going with you."

"No way. It could be dangerous."

"I'm already involved. Are you afraid someone will suspect me of snooping? Maybe even follow me?" She slung her purse over her shoulder and rounded her desk. "Too late. Had that happen last night." She reached past him for the doorknob.

Sean's arm shot out, blocking her path. "What are you talking about? Did someone follow you last night?"

She shrugged. "Maybe."

"That's a yes or no question." He gripped her shoulders. "Inside the Rayburn Building or outside?"

The fear of last night washed over her and took some of the starch out of her backbone. "Outside. A car followed me all the way to my street." At least Sean wouldn't think her crazy for seeing headlights in her mirror.

His fingers tightened on her arms. "You didn't stop at your place, did you?"

The heat of his fingers felt too good, too comforting. TJ pushed his hands aside and stepped back. "No, of course not. I drove by and made a few turns. Finally lost him. Then I went home." She didn't tell him about the headlights in her living room window. Could have been anyone.

"What time did you leave here last night?"

"Around ten-thirty." She started to feel like a witness to a crime—or the criminal herself—and heat rose in her cheeks.

"Did you talk to anyone after you talked to me?"

"Gordon Harris came in after you left."

"Harris?"

TJ's eyes widened. "No. Don't even go there. Gordon mentored me when I started here. I trust him with my life." She thought for a moment. "Oh, Congressman Crane and Congresswoman Malone showed up a little before I left."

Sean didn't respond and TJ didn't like the speculative narrowing of his eyes.

She grabbed her purse and headed for the door. "Come on, we have a business to check out."

Sean reached out and grabbed her arm, sending electric sparks across her skin. "You're not coming."

His words chilled the electrical shocks, and she shrugged his hand away. "Look, get used to the fact that I don't like being told what I can and can't do. If you won't take me with you, I'll follow you. Just try and stop me."

At least by tagging along, she could keep her eye on the mysterious Sean McNeal. Although, if she were honest with herself, she wanted to be around him more than she cared to admit. The scare last night made her want his protection even if she wasn't sure what side he was on.

Sean McNeal, John Newman, whoever he was, was fast crawling beneath her skin again. And that was a dangerous place for her to have him. Hell, she'd rather be scared with Sean McNeal than on her own again with someone stalking her. "Come on." She reached for the doorknob again. "If this place and the people in it have anything to do with the bombing, I want to know."

"If anything goes wrong, promise to stay behind me, will you?" Sean stared hard at her.

Lips pressed together, TJ marched through the doorway, making no such promise.

Chapter Six

"How have you been since Dindi?" As soon as the question was out of Sean's mouth, he regretted asking. He could tell by the dark circles beneath her eyes, she'd had it rough.

TJ sat as far as possible away from him in the compact interior of the nondescript dark pewter sedan he'd chosen as his work vehicle. By the way she worked her lower lip between her teeth, it was obvious she was second-guessing her decision to ride along with him.

"Look, TJ, if we're going to work together on this, we need to talk."

"Who said we were working together?" She darted a frown in his direction. "I'm not *working* with you on anything. I'm just along to keep an eye on you. After all, *you* could be the terrorist."

Anger stabbed at Sean and he took the corner a little faster than he intended, his tires squealing a protest. He had complete control of the car by the time he straightened the wheel. He only wished he had complete control of one ticked-off sandy-blond legislative assistant. The set look on her face boded a rocky time ahead. If he wanted her cooperation, he had some serious feathers to smooth. "I'm sorry I didn't tell you I was alive."

Silence stretched for several long seconds. TJ sat as stiff as a church pew, her face pinched into a tight mask. Okay, so she had every right to be mad. So did he. "I lost a good friend in that explosion. I wanted everyone to think I'd died as well so that I could investigate covertly."

TJ gave no response.

He'd rather she screamed, ranted and raved like any self-respecting hysterical woman. However, from what he'd seen of TJ, that wasn't her way. Anyone who could put up with temperamental politicians when they were in a lather, could handle the death and reappearance of an ex-lover without flying off the handle.

A sigh pulled his attention from the road for a moment.

TJ's shoulders drooped and she leaned back in the seat, closing her eyes. "It doesn't matter. You're alive and no matter how used that makes me feel, I can't bring myself to wish you were dead after all." She shot a menacing glare at him. "Don't ever lie to me again, or you'll wish you *were* dead."

"I won't." He hoped. If it came down to saving her life, he might have to, but he'd cross that bridge when it was burned from beneath him. "So you'll help me when I need it?"

"I didn't say that." She stared out the window, refusing to answer his question. "I, too, will be working to determine who bombed the embassy. Not necessarily with you."

Sean didn't like the sound of that. "We need to work together to solve this. I don't feel comfortable having you snooping around without me."

"Too bad."

"Damn it, TJ. These people are dangerous."

"I'm a big girl. I can make my own decisions without you influencing them."

"Touché." Sean breathed in deeply and let it out. "I promise not to influence your decisions. Just let me know what you're doing, otherwise I can't keep you safe."

"I don't need you to keep me safe." She turned in her seat to face him, her brows low over her forehead. "And one other thing…"

Sean braced himself.

"Understand this. What happened between you and me in Dindi is in the past. As far as I'm concerned, it never happened."

Several more long seconds passed as Sean grappled with how tight the muscles in his chest squeezed. Hadn't he wanted to stay completely focused on the case? She'd given him permission to do just that. Then why did his chest hurt?

"What do we have so far?" TJ's question brought his attention back to the street.

"The money came from a bank in the Caribbean Islands. One of my colleagues hacked into the bank and traced the account to a corporation whose offices are located here in Adams Morgan." He slid the car next to a curb and shifted into Park. Then he glanced at the directions and the numbers on the buildings. "Ready to go find out who spends five hundred thousand dollars to have an embassy bombed?"

TJ's eyes widened. "Five hundred thousand?"

"That was the amount of transfer from the Caribbean bank to Manu's account in Dindi."

"Is Manu the man who actually planted the bomb?"

Sean figured if he was going to get her to buy into his cause, he'd have to share more information than he'd originally intended. "Yes. One of them. I suspect there was another. Neighbors reported a man visiting his apartment."

"Where is Manu now? Why haven't you questioned him?"

"He's dead."

"I see." She sat for a moment, her teeth gnawing at her bottom lip. "Hard to think you can put a price on people's lives."

Sean's grip tightened on the steering wheel. If they had targeted Haddock, Marty and the others were collateral damage. Their lives hadn't been included in the cost. Did that make their lives worthless?

No. Not to a lot of people who'd loved them. Like Kat loved Marty.

"Come on." Sean pushed open his door and stepped out onto the pavement.

"Unless you want to draw attention to yourself, you might consider slowing down and changing your expression," TJ called out behind him. "I'd have worn my jogging shoes if I'd known you were going to run."

He turned, an apology lodging in his throat.

She leaned against a lamppost, pulled off a black pump and dumped a pebble from inside. The slim black skirt she wore reached just above her knees, emphasizing the tight muscles of her calves and trim ankles.

Sean swallowed remembering those ankles wrapped around his waist, their bodies sliding against each other, slick with perspiration. Just one glance at her legs heated his blood and sent him back to a time before the explosion, before Marty's death.

A frown pulled her brows downward. "Have you thought about what you're going to say when you go into this place? Are you just going to march in there and say, 'Hello, I'm Sean McNeal. I'm looking for the guy who blew up the embassy in Dindi?'"

"No, we're going to go in this place and pretend we're there on business."

"Any idea what kind of business?"

"No, but here's the address." He looked up at the sign over the door.

TJ stared, too. "Okay, financial services. I feel the need to invest. How about you, Mr. Newman?"

"I have some cash lying around that needs a place to go. After you, Mrs. Newman."

She shot him a startled look.

Before she could argue, he grabbed her elbow and ushered her through the glass entrance.

A young woman with black hair and deep brown eyes greeted them with a smile. "May I help you?"

"I...uh...yes." TJ stepped forward, darting a glare back at Sean.

Suppressing a grin, he moved to her side and slid an arm around her waist. He read the woman's name tag and jumped in. "Yes, Antonia, is it? My wife and I just came into an inheritance and we need advice on how to invest it."

While the woman pulled out brochures on what the financial service offered in the way of investments, Sean appreciated how fidgety and embarrassed TJ appeared.

"Is this your first time to invest?" Antonia looked

straight into TJ's eyes and smiled. "You don't have to be nervous. We counsel people all the time on how to invest in stocks, bonds and all kinds of commodities, foreign and domestic. Why don't we set up an appointment with one of our trained financial advisors?"

Sean pulled TJ close against him and smiled down into her wide eyes, loving that she was so stunned by his actions, she hadn't uttered a single word. "My wife is concerned about investing and considers it risky. Could you explain to her how it works?"

Although TJ smiled, her lips were tight over her teeth. Okay, so maybe she wasn't so stunned. Angry might be more likely. She leaned into him and ground her heel onto his toes.

"Ouch!" Sean jerked his foot out from under hers. "Careful where you're walking, sweetheart."

"I'm sorry, did I step on your foot, *darling?*" She smiled up at him sweetly, her face all innocence. Definitely angry.

"Only a little." Sean's gaze panned the front room of the office. Mahogany chair-rail molding and elegant paintings of island oases graced the walls of the offices. A door stood open behind the granite receptionist's counter and the lovely Antonia. Sean assumed it led to the back of the building.

"Do you have any advisors available now?" Sean asked.

"No, all our advisors arrange their appointments in advance. I'm sure we could get you on the schedule in the next day or two." She glanced down at a computer monitor on the desk. "I could check for the next availability?"

While TJ worked with the woman behind the counter, Sean noticed a dark-haired man moving through the back room. He stopped to glance at TJ and Sean. Wearing a black silk shirt and dress slacks, he could have been any Washington, D.C., businessman, but for the wary look in his dark eyes. For a long moment he stared at TJ, his eyes narrowing to slits. Why would he stare at her? The man disappeared from sight.

Sean wanted a closer look at the man and the back office area. If he didn't get back there quickly, he might miss the guy altogether. He smiled at Antonia. "Do you have a bathroom I can use? I had two cups of coffee this morning and…well…" He shrugged.

"Sure." She turned and pointed toward the open doorway. "Go through the door and take a right. It's the first door on the left down the short hallway."

"Thanks."

Sean dropped a kiss on TJ's cheek. "Don't go anywhere. Why don't you get all the details and options? I'll be right back."

"But—"

Without waiting for her objection, he hurried behind the counter and through the doorway, pushing it half-closed behind him. If this corporation was responsible for funding the bombing, he would bet Antonia wasn't the kingpin behind it. The man in the back, however, might know something.

Instead of turning right, he turned left in the direction the man had gone. The place appeared deserted; doors open, offices empty except the office two doors down from the reception area. He heard a single voice speaking as if on a telephone. Sean paused in front of the door and shot a glance up and down the hallway. The door muffled the words so much Sean couldn't make out the conversation. Playing ignorant, he pushed the door open.

The man in the black suit leaped from his seat, his fists raised as if ready to defend himself, overreacting for a regular businessman or financial advisor.

"I was looking for the bathroom," Sean lied.

The man's thick, dark brows furrowed and he glared at Sean for a long moment before his fists dropped to his side. "Back the way you came, past the lobby door." He sat back in his chair and waited for Sean to leave, never taking his gaze off him.

"Thanks." Before he closed the door, Sean pressed the photo button on his cell phone, hoping he caught the man's image.

That the man had stared at TJ bugged Sean. In his gut, he knew the guy had recognized her and didn't particularly like that she was there. Sean wanted to know who he was and what he was about. When he emerged from the bathroom, the man's office was open and empty. Sean ducked in and shuffled through the stack of papers littering the desktop. Nothing of interest there. No photos, no notes on his calendar.

After a quick glance over his shoulder, Sean slid open one drawer after another revealing files and office supplies. How long would the guy be gone? Did he risk digging further?

Sean dove in, thumbing through the papers, snapping pictures of names. For the most part, it all looked legitimate.

A door opened and closed near the rear of the building. Footsteps moved closer.

Using a clean tissue from his own pocket, Sean

reached for the stylized pen the man had been using before he'd left the office. Careful not to get his own prints all over it, he tucked it into his pocket and left the office, reaching the doorway back to the reception area as his mystery man emerged from a back room.

He glanced back to see the man staring at him, his eyes narrowed.

Based on the intense look the man had given TJ, Sean thought it best to get her away as soon as possible. He thanked Antonia and herded TJ out.

With the prints and the photographs, he had a little more to go on than when he arrived. He hoped it was enough.

"THANKS FOR DITCHING ME with the counter lady. I learned more about investing than I ever wanted to know." TJ adjusted her seat belt, still cringing over the inane conversation she'd had with Antonia. "You owe me."

"Sorry. I wanted to get a look at someone in the back office."

Her gaze snapped to him, her brown eyes flashing in his peripheral view. "Did you?"

"Did I what?"

"Did you look at someone in the back office?"

"Better than that, I hope. I got a picture of him on my cell phone." He unclipped his phone from his belt and handed it to her.

Pressing several buttons, she found the pictures menu and clicked on the most recent. She clicked through the photos of documents and stopped at a fuzzy picture of a dark-haired man. "And this helps? You can barely make out the documents or the man's facial features."

"Don't need to. My computer guru at the agency will hopefully be able to focus it and get a clear view of the papers. You don't happen to recognize him, do you?"

For a long moment, she stared hard at the fuzzy photo before she shrugged. "No, I can't get much from this picture. All that talk about stocks for a few photographs?" She shook her head. "And you don't even know who he is. Why not the woman behind the counter?"

"I don't think the funding would have come from the minimum wage counter help at a financial services business. But who knows? We'll run this guy first and see if we get a hit."

"Okay, I guess I'll forgive you this time." She snapped his phone shut and settled back against her seat. "Where to? You said something about the agency. Is that where we're headed? Your agency?"

"Yes, ma'am. But first…" He pulled to the side of the road and reached into the glove box.

TJ didn't know what she expected, but a blindfold wasn't it. "Let me guess. You expect me to wear that?"

"If you want to go to the agency. It's standard procedure."

First he'd asked her to trust that he wasn't a bad guy. Now he expected her to put her life in his hands and go into a strange place blindfolded? "No way."

He leaned across her to replace the blindfold in the glove box.

Her curiosity overrode her fear and TJ placed a hand on his arm. "Wait."

His gaze captured hers. "I won't compromise my teammates."

TJ chewed on her bottom lip. "I came along for the ride to keep an eye on you. This goes against my purpose."

"You'll have to trust me." His eyes narrowed. "That's it, isn't it? You still don't trust me." He tossed the bandana back into the glove box and closed it.

"It's not that I don't trust you…well, yes it is. But the truth is I don't know who to trust." Making a quick decision, she yanked the bandana from the glove compartment and tied it around her head. "Okay, are you satisfied? I'm completely in the dark. So what's new?"

A soft chuckle reached her ears. "I shouldn't take you there, but I want you to know, besides the CIA, our team is working the Dindi bombing. We have as much at stake in the outcome as you."

"Then take me to your leader. I don't want to stay in this thing longer than I have to."

Despite her journey into the dark, TJ couldn't help the flutter of excitement. Sean hadn't told her much about what kind of agent he was, and she hadn't had the opportunity to grill him for answers.

The ride from Adams Morgan to wherever they were going didn't take more than fifteen minutes. They slowed to turn and, by the echo of the engine off concrete, they had to be pulling into a parking garage of some sort.

"So who do you really work for?" she asked, straining her sight to see through the thick folds of the bandana. If she'd been smart, she wouldn't have tied it so tightly. Now she paid for her honesty.

"Can't tell you." Sean eased the vehicle to a stop and shifted into Park. "I'm about to show you more than most people in the White House know." His pause stretched for several seconds. "You must promise to keep everything and everyone you see a secret no matter what. Our lives depend on our anonymity."

"I promise, as long as you're not lying to me." TJ fought the urge to squirm in her seat. "You're not FBI and you're not CIA. So what are you?"

"We're the people sent in when all other government organizations aren't quite right for the job."

"Like a super-CIA?"

"Sort of."

"Who sends you in?"

"Top government officials with a desire to ensure the safety and well-being of our country without all the red tape."

"You don't know who they are, do you?" A shiver shook her body at the amount of power such an organization could wield.

"We're not given that information. We're given our missions and we perform them."

"What was your mission in Dindi?"

Sean didn't answer right away. Instead he opened the car door, got out and came around to open hers. "We were to investigate rumors of potential terrorist activities against the United States. Since Congressman Haddock was the prime target for activities against the U.S. we were sent to protect him and discover who might be behind the threat."

The sound of the explosion still rang in TJ's ears. The smell of dust from the crumbled mortar and the acrid scent of demolitions material clung to her senses with the persistence of skunk musk. "You failed that mission, didn't you?"

He leaned in and unclasped her seat belt. "Yes." The one word resonated in the hollow quality of his voice.

"That's why you're so determined to find the backer."
With Sean's assistance, TJ eased out of the car.

He took her elbow and guided her across smooth
concrete. "The price of failure was the lives of Congressman Haddock and many others."

"Including your friend?"

His fingers tightened on her elbow until it hurt. "Yes,
including my friend."

They'd come to a halt and a ding sounded like that of
an elevator. "Don't forget, I lost a friend in that explosion,
too. Don't get me wrong. Most politicians have skeletons
in their closets and Haddock was no different, but he had
good intentions for this country. He didn't deserve to die."

"Nobody did." Sean urged her forward into an
elevator, the floor dipping slightly with their combined
weight. "Come on, I want you to meet someone." Once
inside with the doors closed, he removed the bandana.

TJ rode the elevator in silence. Sean wouldn't have
brought her to his agency unless he trusted her a little.
The purpose and location had to be secret to almost
everyone in the country but a handful of government officials. It didn't make her feel any better. She'd left the
FBI behind to avoid relationships with people in dangerous jobs. Her gut tightened the closer she moved
toward just such a team.

Sean pressed the button for the third floor. Nothing on
the inside of the elevator told her anything about where
they were or what kind of business she would step into.

The elevator doors slid open and they faced a small
vestibule with a solid metal door. Installed on the wall
next to it was an optical scanner. Sean waited while a
bright light scanned his retina.

A shiver slithered down between TJ's shoulder blades. The building reminded her of some of the places she'd been as an FBI agent, with a setup like a scene out of a spy thriller.

"Don't worry. For the most part, the people who work here are harmless."

"I'm not worried," she said, damning her voice for wobbling. His words "for the most part" had her a little wary of who might be behind those doors.

Sean cupped her elbow like he had when he'd escorted her around the streets of Dindi. Who were these people and why hadn't she heard of them up until now?

As the door closed behind them, Sean urged her forward.

He stopped at the first office on his right. "There's someone I want you to meet." He knocked on the door. When a male voice called out to come in, he pushed the door open and stepped in, pulling her behind him.

Inside was a small office with a battered wooden desk, at which a man at least fifteen years older than Sean was seated, a phone to his ear. He held a finger up and continued with his conversation. "Will do. I'll get back to you on that as soon as I get word. Thanks, Jim." He hung up the phone and stood, a frown creasing his forehead when he saw TJ. "Sean, I'm glad you're here. Who's this?"

"Royce, meet TJ Barton." He turned to TJ. "TJ, this is my boss. This organization would be nothing without him."

Her brows rose. "Since I don't know much about the organization, I guess that doesn't mean much."

Royce circled the desk and came to stand in front of TJ. "Mouthy, isn't she?" His lips twitched at the edge.

"I take it you gave her the blindfold treatment and haven't told her any more than she needs to know?"

"You got it." Sean leaned against the door frame. "And she's not too happy about it."

"It's for her own protection as well as ours," Royce said, his gaze running the length of TJ.

TJ's toe tapped against the carpet. "In case you haven't noticed, I'm still standing in front of you."

Royce smiled. "Good to meet you, TJ." He stuck a hand out to shake hers. "Heard a little about you from Sean and Marty. It's nice to put a face to the name."

"Marty?" TJ glanced at Sean, her hand still in Royce's.

"The friend I was telling you about." Sean's lips tightened.

Royce's smile disappeared and his hand tightened on hers. "He was a good friend."

"As was Congressman Haddock." TJ stared straight into Royce's eyes. "So what are you doing about finding the people responsible?"

Royce squeezed her hand and let go. "We have a number of agents on the case."

Sean leaned against the door and crossed one ankle over the other, perfectly relaxed with his boss. "We just got back from checking on that business location. I got a picture of one of the men who worked there. I'll have Tim run a check against known criminals in the area."

"Good, good. Other than that, you got anything else?"

Sean pulled the tissue-wrapped pen from his pocket. "I got this from the guy in the picture. Could you run prints on it?"

TJ frowned. He hadn't bothered to tell her that little bit of news. What else was he hiding from her?

"Sure will. Now, if you'll excuse me, I have a lunch date with a senator." Royce held out his hand to TJ. "Nice to meet you, TJ. Take care of Sean for us. He's a good guy."

Not he's a good agent, but he's a good guy. The words warmed TJ's insides. Her initial impression of Sean from their stay in Dindi was that he was a good guy. But she'd already been fooled once.

So, he had his reasons. She didn't have to like them.

"Sean!" A woman with long, black hair and ice-blue eyes came out of the office on their left and wrapped her arms around Sean in a tight squeeze. "I didn't think you'd be back in the office for several days."

"Hi, Kat." Sean set her at arms length and stared down into her eyes, his expression soft.

A stab of something that felt like jealousy pinched at TJ's heart. She shook the feeling away as soon as it surfaced. Jealousy had nothing to do with solving the case.

"Kat, I want you to meet someone." Sean turned her toward TJ. "TJ, this is Kat." Sean still held the woman's hands in his own. "Marty's widow."

TJ looked deeper into the woman's shadowed eyes. Having witnessed the bombing and experienced the anguish of Sean's "death" over the past month, she could understand what Kat was going through. A lump formed in her throat at the memory of finding Sean's bed empty in the hospital. "I'm sorry," was all she could manage.

"It's okay." The dark-haired woman shrugged, the muscles in her throat working to swallow before she went on. "Some days are better than others."

Sean pressed a brotherly kiss to the top of her head

and hugged her again, his eyes suspiciously shiny. "Is Tim in the office today?"

Kat laughed softly. "Where else would he be?" She nodded toward the far corner. "He's in his usual spot in the computer lab."

"Thanks, Kat. I'll call you later." Sean squeezed her hand and let go.

The widow disappeared back into the office and closed the door behind her.

"Kat's an agent, too?" TJ asked.

Sean nodded. "One of the best."

TJ stared at the closed door, her heart going out to the woman behind it. "You sure Marty wasn't faking it like you did?"

"I wish, but no. I performed CPR on him for twenty minutes. He never revived. Marty was my friend, I'd have given my life for him." He gave one more brooding glance at the office door. "Come on. I want Tim to do his magic on this picture and we need to get back to work." Gone was the sad look, and in its place was a determined set to his jaw.

If anyone could find who did this to Marty and Congressman Haddock, Sean would be the man. "So how can I help in this investigation?"

"The best way you can help is to do as little as possible."

"Then why did you introduce me to your team?"

"I wanted you to know why it's so important to me."

"And it's not as important to me?" Anger surged. He wanted her help but he didn't.

"I didn't say that."

"Well, it is as important to me as to you. I want to know who bombed that building just as badly as you do."

"Look, TJ. The more questions you ask of others, the more suspicion you cast on yourself and the more dangerous it gets."

"I can take care of myself." She turned to face him. "Besides, two people working this case from the inside has to be better than one."

"Let me be the judge of how you can help. In the meantime, don't ask any more questions."

TJ stared straight ahead, seething at his high-handedness. She'd be damned if she sat back and did nothing.

Chapter Seven

Sean entered the office a few minutes before Congresswoman Malone. He wanted to spend time questioning Gordon Harris about his conversation with TJ last night, but the man wasn't in. Sean really wanted to know if Gordon had been the one to follow her home. That someone had tailed TJ had him worried.

When Congresswoman Malone strode through the doorway, the other staffers shuffled papers as if her very presence made them nervous.

Gordon Harris hurried to keep up with her. "I have that report for the Budget Committee on your desk."

"Damn the Budget Committee." Congresswoman Ann Malone jerked to a stop, every hair on her dark brown, neatly coiffed head remained in place, as if they didn't dare get out of line. Red flags of color rode high on her cheekbones and her eyes flashed like lightning. "As soon as we left the Appropriations Committee meeting, Congressman Crane headed straight for the rowing club."

"He rows every day," Gordon offered. "Just like some people jog."

"Damned rowing club. It's as bad as golf. If you don't play, you don't hear about or make the deals." She speared Sean with her gaze. "John, do you row or play golf?"

Sean shook his head. "If you mean do I belong to the rowing club, no, ma'am. And I don't see much purpose in spending four hours of a day hitting a ball around a field."

"I knew there was something I liked about you. And drop the ma'am. You can call me Ann." The congress-woman smiled, making her plain features almost pretty.

Her campaign photos were taken with her smiling, the green of her eyes enhanced and a Jackie O attention to detail with her wardrobe. Designer business suits cut to fit her trim body and matching shoes with heels not too low as to be frumpy and not high enough for a street-walker. She was the image of a successful politician.

Sean had studied the dossier S.O.S. had put together on Ann Malone. Forty-seven, married, no children, husband basically out of the picture, a successful busi-nessman stuck running a company in New York for the majority of the year.

From the day she'd stepped on the campaign trail, Malone had orchestrated her rise to Congress with preci-sion. Not until she'd been elected did she run into problems climbing the food chain. More established con-gressmen held the power and made sure Congresswoman Malone and any other upstart legislators knew their places.

Sean had glimpsed Malone's frustration with the system and predicted that if she didn't learn to play the game, she wouldn't get far with the senior members of the House. Especially with Representative Thomas

Crane who had stepped into Haddock's position as chairman of the Appropriations Committee, a detail that seemed to grate on Malone's nerves.

"Did I receive anything from a Tab Browning in the morning distro?" she asked.

"A courier delivered an envelope this morning marked confidential, with no return address. Is that what you're looking for?" He'd signed for it with lots of people around or he'd have taken a look inside.

Her green eyes gleamed and her lips curled on the ends. "Yes. Where is it?"

"It's on your desk."

Malone turned without another word and closed the office door behind her.

Must be important information.

Being undercover for a detail-oriented congress-woman cut into the time Sean needed to pursue leads. Thank goodness the congresswoman was due to attend a cocktail party at five-thirty that evening. He'd arranged a meeting time with TJ after seven when most of the staff had gone home or to the bars in Adams Morgan. TJ promised to sneak him into Haddock's and Crane's offices to sort through documents. Maybe they'd find a program or a bill Haddock had planned to champion that would make someone desperate enough to kill the older congressman.

Although he hated to drag TJ into the investigation, he realized how much easier movement through the offices would be with her keyed access. TJ agreed, albeit reluctantly. Though she wanted to nail whoever funded the bomber as much as he did, her sense of honesty and loyalty made her hesitate. He'd get her to let him in, and then he'd take it from there, performing the investigation himself. That way, if he got caught, he wouldn't take her down with him.

Sean glanced at his watch. Five minutes to five. He hadn't seen TJ in only two hours and it felt a lot longer. The problem with being undercover was that you had to at least appear to be performing the job you'd been hired to do. He preferred to be digging for clues instead of proofing speech notes for Malone or reminding her of meetings and engagements she was scheduled to attend. Speaking of which…

Sean knocked on the representative's door.

"Yes?"

He opened the door and ducked his head in. "Ma'am, you have the cocktail party on your schedule. Shouldn't you be leaving?"

Seated behind her desk, she glanced over a pair of reading glasses at the clock on the far wall. "Oh yes, of course. The Daughters of the American Revolution social. And it's Ann. Please call me Ann. Ma'am makes me feel old." She shuffled what looked like photographs into the envelope and slipped the packet into her desk. "Are you headed home?"

"I have a few items to file and that speech to revise. It shouldn't take more than an hour." He didn't plan on leaving until after his rendezvous with TJ later that evening. But Ann Malone didn't have to know that.

"Fine." Instead of looking at him, she looked through him as if she were miles ahead. "Don't stay too late."

"Yes, ma'am." He caught himself. "I mean, Ann."

As soon as she left the office and cleared the hallway, Sean slipped back into her office. Curiosity lead him to the envelope she'd tucked into her desk drawer. She'd been viewing photographs. Of what?

Testing the drawer, he cursed beneath his breath. Locked.

Using a hard plastic tool he carried in his jacket for just such an occasion, Sean jimmied the lock and the drawer slid open. The envelope sat on top of the files within.

Quickly, he rifled through the contents, at least a dozen pictures of two men. One of them looked like Congressman Crane, in jogging shorts, rowing a two-man kayak on what appeared to be the Potomac or the C&O Canal, based on the buildings and bridges visible in the background.

Was Congresswoman Malone so desperate to know what went on out there she'd hire a private investigator to spy on Crane? Sean didn't recognize the other man in the pictures. He pocketed the clearest shot of the man and Crane together and slid the remaining photos back into the envelope. After he replaced the pictures in the desk drawer, he slipped the lock back in place.

Maybe TJ would know who the other man was. He left Malone's office and headed down the hall to Haddock's office suite.

The door was open, but TJ wasn't there. Gordon Harris stood beside her desk loading a stack of files into her in-box. When he turned to face him, he smiled. "Hey, John, looking for TJ?"

"Yes. Is she still here?"

"You just missed her." The man laid the last of the folders and memos in TJ's in-box and then collected a stack from her out-box before he joined Sean at the door. "How's it going? Malone making you crazy yet?"

"Not so bad."

"She's a very demanding woman and she can dole out some severe tongue-lashings if she thinks you're undermining her authority. Trust me. I've seen it happen. And she's not afraid of firing someone on the spot."

"Sounds like a woman who knows her mind."

"No doubt. She and Crane had a shouting match after the committee meeting today."

"Anything I should be aware of to avoid tripping one of her buttons?" Sean asked.

"She's got it in for one of his pet projects."

"Which one?"

"He's been pushing the Arobo Millennium Challenge proposal and she's not too happy with it. Malone and Haddock were backing Dindi until Haddock died in the bombing. She and Crane made a lot of noise outside the committee's meeting room."

The Millennium Challenge deal wasn't dead and it might be something he should learn more about. First, he wanted to know more about Gordon's whereabouts after TJ left the building. "You worked pretty late last night, didn't you?"

Gordon shrugged. "No more than usual."

Vague. The hair on the back of Sean's neck rose. Not exactly the answer he'd wanted. Gordon had been one of the last people to talk to TJ before she left last night. He could have been the one to follow her.

"Malone called me in to find a missing document."

"Did she come in late as well?" Sean's brows rose.

"Oh yeah. She and Congressman Crane came in and gave me another hour of work to do before I could go. I didn't get out of here until after eleven."

"Do you always work that late?" If Gordon didn't

leave until after eleven, he couldn't be the person who'd followed TJ.

Gordon nodded. "I'm Malone's legislative director. If she says jump, I jump."

"No family, huh?"

"None. Unless you call Congresswoman Malone family."

"Doesn't give you much of a life."

"Maybe not, but she's been good to me. I'd do anything for her."

Anything? Would he kill for the congresswoman? Sean looked at Gordon, carefully reading his body language and everything about him. The man didn't look like a killer.

Gordon tucked the stack of papers under his arm. "I'd better get back to my office. I have a lot to do and reports to get back to TJ before I leave."

TJ. His pulse quickened. "You said I just missed her? Will she be coming back soon?"

"No, she left for the day. She cut out about fifteen minutes ago saying something about jogging."

Jogging after being tailed last night? From Gordon's account, he didn't leave the building until well after TJ last night. Someone else had to have followed her. What if that someone was still watching her?

By the time he looked up her home address, he'd miss her. Without trying to seem too obvious Sean walked out of TJ's office with Gordon. "Where are the good places to jog around here?"

"I prefer Rock Creek Park myself. TJ takes the towpath along the canal in Georgetown."

The towpaths were his preference as well and he was familiar with them.

"Thanks, Gordon. I'm calling it a day. See ya tomorrow?"

"Hey, you want to catch a drink on Friday? I'll introduce you to some of the other members of the staff."

"Sure. Later." He was already halfway down the hall, calculating the amount of time it would take to change and get to the jogging trails along the C&O Canal. Even if he got down there in the next ten minutes, he had no guarantee of finding TJ on the path. He'd see her at seven that evening, but suddenly he felt the need to make sure she was all right.

What concerned Sean most was the fact that someone in D.C. pulled the trigger to have the embassy bombed. What if the killer had found out TJ was looking for him? What if that killer was the same person tailing her last night? She'd make an easy target on the jogging trail.

Had she been asking questions about the bombing? Since TJ was one of the only survivors, did the killer consider her a threat? Why, after a month, would the killer target her unless the CIA's questioning or TJ's questioning set off alarm bells?

He continued walking toward his car, his pace quickening until he ran.

THE SUN ANGLED LOW, sending long shadows through the vegetation and trees lining the jogging trail. Except for the rumble of traffic on the roads surrounding the area and the occasional blare of a horn, the river was silent. All TJ could hear were the sounds of her breathing and the rhythmic beat of her shoes hitting the pavement.

Normally, she exercised in the morning in order to

keep on a routine workout schedule. The end of the workday as a legislative assistant seldom allowed for a set time to work out. Many days she worked late into the evening checking facts that needed clarification or a project that demanded immediate attention before the next day. But tonight she didn't have anyone hounding her for a report or asking her to stay late to finish writing a speech. Leaving her desk clean, she slipped out of the office while the coast was clear, avoiding Congresswoman Malone's door and Sean McNeal.

She needed the time away from the Rayburn Building to clear her head and think. No, she wanted the time away from McNeal to allow her to think *straight*.

Their trip to meet Sean's boss and some of his teammates brought back too many memories of her days in the FBI with more than just a nostalgic tug. She'd loved the challenge of the cases she worked, liked solving the puzzles of who-done-it. She missed the camaraderie of her fellow agents. But when her partner took a bullet to the spine, she'd reevaluated her life and career choice. Ultimately, she'd left the Bureau, cutting herself off from all her friends and coworkers there. She'd given it all up rather than face the constant reminder that it could happen to any one of them. She didn't think she could face that kind of loss again.

As a legislative assistant the only deaths she faced were the random car accidents or heart attacks. Her actions or inactions wouldn't cause the death or permanent paralysis of someone who was like family. So she thought. Until Congressman Haddock's death in the explosion. Had TJ been with him, she would have died, too.

A month of soul-searching yielded the right answer.
She couldn't turn back time, and she couldn't have done
anything different that would have saved Haddock's life
or her partner's legs. Wishing she'd died along with
Haddock was a defeatist attitude she refused to take.

With thoughts of Sean, Haddock and her past
tumbling around in her mind, she didn't hear the other
set of running shoes until they were right behind her.
The sun had dipped behind a cloud on its descent to the
horizon, throwing D.C. into a premature dusk, length-
ening shadows until they merged.

Many businessmen and women jogged the towpaths
early in the morning and after work. Why the sound of
shoes following her on the path should bother her this
time, she didn't know. She sped up in an attempt to put
some distance between her and the person following.
The footsteps dogged her, matching her pace.

As she rounded a curve, TJ risked a glance backward.
Whoever followed stayed just out of sight around another bend in the trail.

TJ slowed and the person behind her slowed.

Her heart rate ratcheted up several notches and had
nothing to do with her level of exertion and everything to
do with fear. Unfortunately, she was headed the wrong
way on the towpath. If she wanted to get to the relative
safety of the city streets, she needed to run in the opposite
direction. The farther she ran, the darker it grew and the
farther away from help she moved. She should have turned
around a long time ago and headed back to her apartment.

Weighing her options, TJ decided to take a plunge
and duck through the bushes to the paved trail. First she
wanted a little more distance between them. She broke

out in an all-out run. By the time she reached a point on the trail with a break in the brush, her lungs neared bursting and she couldn't hear anything over the blood banging against her eardrums. She held her breath and listened past the noise of her own pulse and the steady pounding of her shoes on the packed earth.

That's when he hit her from behind, knocking her to the ground. TJ let out a scream before a hand clamped over her mouth and the weight of a man landed on her back, forcing the rest of the air from her lungs.

She lay facedown on the ground in the dark, tackled by a stranger and no one knew where she was.

TJ was in trouble. Then she heard Sean's voice over the sound of the stranger's breath in her ears.

"TJ!" His voice sounded blessedly near.

Unable to even squirm beneath the weight on her back, she kicked her heel upward, making contact with some portion of the man's body.

The man grunted and shoved her face into the ground so hard she snorted dirt up her nose.

"TJ!"

Her captor jerked her by the hair and smashed her face into the dirt. Then he leaped to his feet and ran.

"TJ!"

Sean raced around the corner and almost tripped over her inert body before he saw her. "TJ? What happened?"

She rolled to her back and pushed to a sitting position, sucking several long breaths into her lungs before she answered. "Someone hit me from behind."

"Are you okay?"

She brushed the dirt from her cheek. "I think so."

"Where'd he go?"

She looked back over her shoulder. "That way."

"Stay here and don't get up." He raced after her attacker.

"Stay here? I don't think so." TJ rose and trotted after him.

As she rounded the bend in the trail, she almost ran into Sean headed back her way.

"Why did you come back?"

Sean shook his head, his lips pressing into a straight line. "I figured you wouldn't stay put, and I was afraid he might try to circle back and finish what he started."

TJ planted her fists on her hips. "I can take care of myself."

"Yeah, I can see that."

So, she'd screwed up. She should have known better than to jog alone so close to dark. "We have to catch him, Sean. He might be our killer." TJ didn't wait for a response and took off after her attacker.

Sean raced after her. "You sure you're up to this?"

"You bet." The grit in her teeth made her mad and she'd be damned if she let the man get away with catching her off guard. She'd take him down if it was the last thing she did.

Chapter Eight

TJ ran alongside Sean, her eyes straining against the darkening sky. The man had the head start. They probably wouldn't catch him, but they had to try.

She didn't like to think what might have happened if Sean hadn't come along when he did, so she pushed the thought aside and picked up the pace.

The excitement of the chase was one of the things she'd missed most about being an FBI agent. After long hours of digging through clues until coming up with the right suspect, she liked to be the one to finally corner the criminal and bring him in.

Legislative assistants didn't have that kind of exhilaration unless you counted the occasional bomb threat in the building. The adrenaline rush of catching a potential criminal and bringing him to justice…now that had exhilaration written all over it. And TJ thrilled at the blood racing through her veins. Damn she'd missed this.

They came up on a clear view of the C&O Canal. Just as she spotted her attacker, Sean caught her around the middle and dragged her back into the bushes.

TJ struggled to breathe with her heart hammering

against her chest. Not from her earlier fear of rape and murder, more, to her consternation, from her reaction to Sean's embrace.

"Look." Sean pointed through the brush.

Not far ahead, a tall, dark man in running sweats and shoes leaped off the trail and down to the river. A dark red canoe with a large gold crest on the side rested against the bank. The man sitting in the canoe wore a hooded sweatshirt that obscured his face.

Her attacker climbed into the canoe and pushed it away from the shore. The man with the paddle dug his oar into the water. The boat skimmed across the canal's surface, headed back toward the Francis Scott Key Memorial Bridge.

TJ performed an about-face and jogged after them. They were moving a lot faster than she and Sean could jog and she lost sight as brush blocked her view of the water.

When the trail curved toward the river again, the vegetation opened, giving them another clear view of the waterway. The steel-gray water of the C&O Canal proved little resistance to the lone canoe as it glided past, pulling away from them.

TJ poured all she had into keeping up. Ultimately, the vegetation cleared and they were out in the open, running along the trail parallel to the canal. More concerned about catching her attacker than the risk to her life, TJ didn't slow, still a good football field length behind the two men.

As the canoe neared the bridge, the man paddling steered toward the bank, sliding up onto the shore. Before the boat came to a stop, the attacker got out and stood beside the vessel.

When the man in the canoe leaned forward, his hood no longer obstructed his chin and facial features as much as before.

TJ slowed to get a look at him in what little light was left from the evening sky. At that moment, both men glanced her way. The man in the boat pointed at her and said something to the man standing on land.

Her attacker scowled at them and said something to the man in the boat.

"I've seen that face before," TJ said.

"So have I." Sean's voice sounded grim.

Where had she seen it? The memory nagged at her without surfacing fully.

The man in the boat handed the guy onshore something that looked like—

"Crud, he's got a gun." Adrenaline revived the oxygen-starved cells in her blood and TJ leaped forward.

Sean moved so that his body blocked her from the man's aim. "Run, TJ, as fast as you can—"

A loud crack exploded behind her.

Sean grabbed her hand and ran faster, hurrying her along.

TJ could barely keep up, her lungs screaming for air.

As soon as buildings came into view, Sean turned left and they ran up the short incline to K Street, blending into the pedestrian traffic filling the sidewalks. Slowing to a quick walk, they wended their way through the people and crossed to the other side of the street. TJ darted a look backward and couldn't see the guy tailing them. And didn't really want to.

Sean hooked an arm around her waist and pulled her into a dark alley, leading her to the end and around to the back of a building. Not until they were out of sight of the busy street did TJ think to breathe.

Then she collapsed against aged bricks and hauled huge gulps of air into her burning lungs.

"Are you all right?" Sean stood next to her, running his hand down her back.

"Yes, as soon as I can…breathe." His touch was warm and reassuring at the same time as it was disturbing. After their flight from danger, her blood moved too fast. The added stimulus of Sean's hand on her back…well…was more stimulus than she could handle and breathing wasn't getting any easier. After several more deep breaths, she straightened, her legs wobbling.

Sean's hand slipped down her back and fell away.

TJ missed the solid pressure. "Okay. I'm okay now," she said, not really feeling steady, but not willing to admit it to Sean.

"Good. Because I'm not." He grabbed her shoulders and shook her. "Don't go running by yourself again until this is all over, do you hear me?"

She stared up at him, a stubborn streak stiffening her back. But after having her face smashed into the dirt, she didn't feel quite as invincible. She sighed and leaned into him. "Okay, I promise."

"Good." He jerked her into his arms. "When I heard you'd left the office to go jog—" He inhaled and let out a long breath, ruffling the hair by her temple.

He'd been afraid for her. Warmth filled the inside of her chest and she grasped the light cotton jersey of his T-shirt, her fingers bunching it in her fists, holding him close. This is where she'd wanted to be ever since she discovered Sean alive in D.C. In his arms.

When he set her at arm's length, she stared up into his eyes. "What was that for?" Was that her voice, the breathless whisper barely audible over the busy street?

"I couldn't help it. You scared me and just in case you didn't already know it, you're incredibly sexy when you're sweating like a horse."

If she thought her knees were shaking before, they all but gave way at the teasing gleam in Sean's eyes. "You sure know how to compliment a girl." She stared down at her perspiration-soaked shirt and back up at him and smiled. "I have to admit that was fun."

"I bet you made a great agent."

All laughter fled in an instant and she stepped away from his touch. Of course he'd know she'd been an FBI agent. Any agent worth his salt would have learned as much as he could about all those involved in the Dindi trip. Especially the one he'd slept with. It still galled her that she'd been a convenient cover for him. "I left that life a long time ago," she muttered as she turned and headed toward the alley.

Sean caught up and fell in step beside her. "Why? What happened?"

Now wasn't the time to go into her reasons for leaving the FBI. Given the current situation, her reasons didn't seem that important. "We need to get back if you want to go through Haddock's and Crane's offices tonight. I'm not thrilled with the idea of letting you in, so don't be late or I'll change my mind."

SEAN FLAGGED A CAB and delivered TJ back to her apartment in Georgetown where he walked her to the door.

After TJ had been followed the night before and attacked along the towpath, Sean didn't want to leave her.

Other than a few specifics about their planned meeting, she didn't say much. The silence stretched long and cold like a dreary winter day. And she didn't explain why she went from laughter to an expressionless mask in a matter of a few words.

What had he said? Something about her being an agent. Was that it? Did she still hold it against him for going undercover in Dindi?

Whatever TJ's problem, she wasn't sharing.

After he'd held her in his arms, he didn't want her at a distance anymore. He wanted to hold her on a regular basis, to run his fingers through her hair and forget himself and everything else in her.

A man had attacked TJ tonight and the thought set Sean's pulse racing. He couldn't let anything else happen to her.

TJ fished for her keys in the pocket of her sweat jacket without looking up at him. "Want to meet at eight instead of seven? I need a shower."

"Eight's fine." The knot in his gut grew with each passing minute of this investigation and he still had no real suspects to show for his work. "I'll pick you up then."

"No need, I have my own car."

"Look, you were attacked tonight. I shouldn't be leaving you alone."

She crossed her arms over her chest. "I can take care of myself. I was trained in self-defense."

"I did my homework. I know you were trained by the FBI." He gripped her arms. "Tessa, sometimes self-defense isn't enough. Not if a killer is determined."

Her brow furrowed, TJ shook off his hands. "Well, it's good enough for me." She poked the key at the lock, missing the first time. "Just leave me alone." Was that a wobble in her voice? Was the tough TJ on the verge of tears?

Sean closed his hand over hers, inserted the key and unlocked the door. When he'd pushed her inside and closed the door behind them, he grabbed her shoulders, turning her to face him. "What's wrong?" Sean wasn't moving until she answered.

"Nothing." Her body grew rigid beneath his hands.

"Don't give me that. I know you're mad about something." He shook her gently. "Tell me, Tessa."

"Don't call me Tessa." She jerked free and turned her back on him.

"Okay, TJ, what made you mad?"

She inhaled and let it out before she faced him. "Answer one question for me and I'll let the matter drop."

"Okay, shoot." He crossed his arms over his chest.

"In Dindi, was sleeping with me part of your cover?"

"What?"

"You heard me."

So that was it. She was worried that what they had in Dindi was all a lie. "No." TJ had meant a lot more to him than a cover for the operation. When he reached for her again, she backed away.

"I said I'd let it drop. I keep my word." She pushed a hand through her hair. "Now, about my attacker and the man in the canoe."

Sean wanted to continue the Dindi conversation, but one look at TJ's face told him that dialogue was over. "What about them? Did you recognize them?"

"I didn't get a good enough look at the man in the canoe, but I know I've seen the guy who attacked me." She tapped her finger to her chin and stared at a painting on the wall. "I just can't remember where."

"I recognized the guy who shot at us as the same man from the financial services place. It's the other guy I couldn't make out."

"At least we saw one of them."

"Could the guy in the canoe be the same guy in this photo?" From his sweatpants pocket, he pulled the rumpled picture of a man in a suit talking to Congressman Crane and handed it to her.

TJ stared at the picture for a few moments before shaking her head. "I didn't get a good look at him. The guy in the picture is Jason Frazier. He's a lobbyist for Troy Oil." She turned the photo over. "Where'd you get this?" She handed him the photo.

"From an envelope in Malone's office."

She didn't even blink at his confession. "Why is Malone carrying around photos of Congressman Crane and a lobbyist? Lobbyists are always meeting with the members. There's nothing unusual about that."

"I don't know. But I think it's really important to find out who our man from St. Croix Financial Services is as well as the guy in the canoe. Especially since they thought we were interesting enough to shoot at us."

"The canoes are available to anyone from a number of outfitters. We could check the records at the rental shops. Did your computer tech at the office ever get back with you on the cell-phone pictures or the finger prints?"

Sean pulled his phone from his other pocket and

checked for messages. None. "No. But if you'll give me a minute, I'll call."

TJ glanced at her watch. "It's after six. Would he still be there?"

"Tim lives at the office. If he's not upstairs watching the Sci Fi Channel, he's at his computer hacking his way into more information." He punched the number for the S.O.S. office and waited, then entered Tim's extension.

"This is Tim." The young man's voice sounded muffled. "Hang on. Let me put you on speaker. Can't hold and type at the same time… There… Is this Sean?"

"Hey, Tim. Yeah, it's me. Anything on the pictures from my cell phone or the fingerprints?"

"We got a match on the picture of a local businessman named Trey Masterson from St. Croix Financial Services."

"Nothing exciting in that. That was the name on the papers he signed." Sean sensed there was more. "What about the fingerprints?"

"That's the interesting thing. We sent the fingerprints over to our contact at the FBI and they ran it through the Integrated Automated Fingerprint Identification System and came up with a match. I was just about to call you."

"Great. Who is the real Trey Masterson?"

TJ leaned closer, pressing her ear to the back of the phone. The scent of spring flowers clogged Sean's ability to think.

"Eddy Smith," Tim answered.

Sean shook his head. "Who's Eddy Smith?"

"He's got a short rap sheet for crimes such as fraud and embezzlement. Nothing major. But it's who he hangs out with that has me concerned. My contacts at the FBI tell me he's been spotted with Rick Molini in the past three weeks."

"Isn't Molini connected to the mob?"

"Yup." Tim paused, then added, "Molini's been known as a gun for hire. But then again, the mob might need financial advice just like the rest of us."

Right. Just like the rest of us. Sean doubted Eddy was talking with Rick about that kind of investment. "Thanks, Tim. That gives us something to go on."

"You're welcome. Let me know if you need anything else." Tim hung up.

TJ gasped and tugged at Sean's sleeve. "Let me see that picture on your phone again."

"Why?"

"I think I remember where I saw him." She grabbed his phone out of his hands and flipped it open, scrambling through the menu to find the picture. When she did, her face paled.

Sean gripped her beneath her elbows. "Where? At the St. Croix Financial Services office?"

"No." She looked up at him, her eyes wide. "I saw him in Dindi."

"What do you mean?"

TJ drew in a deep breath and let it out. "He was dressed as a businessman. He left the embassy right before it exploded."

SEAN LEFT TJ AT her apartment with strict instructions not to let anyone in and not to leave until he came to collect her. After returning to the S.O.S. complex to shower, he slipped into the business-casual clothing fitting a staff assistant working after hours: black polo shirt and chinos. Anxious for more information on Eddy Smith and Rick Molini, he'd stopped at the computer lab before heading back to TJ's apartment. Royce and Tim looked up from a monitor.

Without preamble, Sean launched into his questions. "What more did you find on Smith?"

"Nothing more than what we had before. Now, Molini is a different subject. He's suspected in several bombing attempts on government facilities stateside. The FBI have been all over his ass, searching for evidence to nail him." Royce tapped his pen in his palm. "As far as they know, Molini hasn't tried anything in foreign territory."

"Why is he still on the streets and why is he meeting with Smith?" Sean demanded.

Royce sat on the edge of a table, his arms crossed over his chest. "From the court records and news clippings, they never found enough evidence to make charges stick to Molini. He usually covers his tracks pretty well."

Sean's lips pressed together. "TJ says she saw Smith leaving the embassy right before the bombing. If he's a friend of Molini, who's to say Molini hasn't trained him on what he knows? All we have to do is prove he was in Dindi and he knows Molini. That information plus the fact he attacked TJ tonight on the towpaths while she was jogging, should be enough to bring him in."

Royce frowned. "Molini couldn't have left the country. The FBI would have him on every watch list if he tried to leave the country. Makes sense to send someone they wouldn't suspect."

Tim looked up from a one-year-old news headline featuring Rick Molini being acquitted on charges of bombing a government facility in North Carolina. "And TJ Barton wasn't supposed to arrive at the embassy late, but she did and she can place him."

"All the more reason for him to get rid of her before she tells the feds." Royce shook his head.

Sean paced the floor, wishing he'd stayed with TJ. "I don't like it. How soon can we bring him in?"

"We can't."

The tenuous hold Sean had on his temper slipped and he slammed his hand on the table. "What do you mean we can't?" Computer monitors rattled and Tim's keyboard jumped.

"Hey. This is delicate equipment." Tim glared at Sean.

Royce raised his hand. "Think about it, Sean. The man's a hired gun. We have to find who hired him before we can bring him in."

Sean bit down on his retort, the muscles in his jaw twitching. "Damn it. TJ's a walking target."

"So are you. He saw you with TJ tonight. I don't like TJ being a target any better than you do. But we will find out who backed the bombing. For Marty's sake and everyone else who died in that building."

"Are you saying TJ could be collateral damage?"

"No." Royce shook his head. "I know you're on it and will stick to her like glue to keep her safe."

He hoped he could. "The woman has a mind of her own."

"Yeah. And who better to read it than someone really close to her?" Royce's brows rose.

His eyes narrowing, Sean couldn't refute Royce.

"Now." Royce clapped his hands together. "We need to find out who the other man in the canoe was."

A few moments later, Tazer stepped into the doorway of the computer lab, her sleek black dress and high heels incongruous with the office setting.

"Going on a date?" Sean asked.

Tazer's gaze scraped him from toe to top, then one slim brown brow winged upward. "Think I'd dress like this for a date?"

"On assignment, huh?"

She nodded and turned her attention to Royce. "You need me?"

"Yeah, tomorrow I need you to find a canoe-rental company." Royce glanced at Sean for the specifics.

He told her about the dark red canoe with the fancy gold crest stenciled on the sides.

Royce straightened from his perch on the table. "Get a list of all the people renting canoes this afternoon and of any turned in late."

"Sure." Her gaze connected with Sean's. "Is this for you, Sean?"

"For the Dindi bombing case and Marty," Sean said.

Tazer's lips thinned. "Anything for Marty and Kat. You can count on me." She turned her attention to Royce. "Is that all you wanted?"

The older man nodded. "It's enough for now."

"Then I'll call it a night."

"Tazer...thanks," Sean said.

"Any time." With the grace of a leopard, she pivoted on a stiletto heel and walked away.

Once she'd disappeared, Royce pinned Sean with one of those read-through-you-in-a-second looks. "You and TJ, how're things going on that front?"

"Fine." *Nothing I want to tell you at this time.* He

wasn't ready to admit he was getting too involved all over again. If Royce thought he was having a tough time focusing, he'd pull him from the case and assign someone else to protect TJ. And Sean couldn't let that happen. TJ was in up to her eyeballs and he couldn't let her fly this bird alone.

"Well, if you need to talk about anything, you know where to find me."

"Thanks, boss." Sean escaped before Royce could ask any more questions he wasn't ready to answer.

TJ FUMBLED WITH HER identification badge as she slowly passed through the X-ray scanner and the magnetometer.

The Capitol Police officer manning the scanner smiled. "Working late?"

"Yes, sir. Got a report due by morning." She'd rehearsed the line several times on her drive over to the building. Sean had followed her car, remaining right on her tail all the way. He'd stayed in the parking garage, insisting they enter at different times to avoid suspicion or complications. They'd meet at her office in fifteen minutes.

His commanding attitude chafed at her sense of independence. As a former member of the Bureau, TJ knew what to do and how to handle moving around a city alone. The most important key to staying alive was remaining observant at all times.

Eddy Smith shouldn't have been able to sneak up on her on the jogging trail. Her skills must be getting rusty or she'd been buried too deep in her own world to hear him coming. Probably the similar feeling Sean had about the bombing in Dindi. TJ knew how dangerous distractions could be.

Once through the entrance, TJ hurried to her office. She still had access to Haddock's files and hoped to go through them before Sean showed up. Although, having worked with Haddock's staff for the past three years, she'd been in and out of the documents stored in his file cabinets and had never seen anything strange.

With the explosion taking place in Dindi during the Millennium Challenge negotiations, TJ couldn't think of any other motive for the bombing other than to get Haddock out of the way for other proposals. In the grand scheme of government grants and funding, one MC application didn't seem worth killing a congressman over. Maybe they were overreacting and the bombing was as simple as a terrorist organization wanting to make a statement against Americans in general, not necessarily Congressman Haddock in particular. Then why had money been sent from the U.S. via the Caribbean account to the terrorist's account?

In her own office, TJ dug in a drawer for the mini flashlight she kept in case of power outages, and stuck it in her pants pocket. She made a quick sweep of Haddock's office suite to make sure no one was there and then she ducked into the filing room and rummaged through the cabinets.

TJ read through the Millennium Challenge documents she helped prepare prior to the trip to Dindi. Nothing jumped out until she reached a letter from Prime Minister Abediayi addressed to Congressman Haddock. Scanning through the stilted pleasantries, she stopped when she got to the real reason for the letter. TJ's hand shook as she read it word for word.

Oil engineers assure us there are ample reserves off the coast of Dindi. With the MC funding, we hope to further explore this natural resource.

TJ looked up and stared at the photo taken of Haddock, Crane, Malone and several other members of the Appropriations Committee. Was someone getting a kickback from an oil company?

The door opened behind her and she spun, dropping into a fighting crouch.

Chapter Nine

Gordon Harris held his hands up. "Whoa, tiger. It's just me."

"Oh, Gordon." She inhaled, then gradually let the breath out hoping to slow her erratic heartbeat. "How's it going?"

Gordon reached out and touched a hand to her face. "I'm fine, it's you I'm worried about. You look feverish."

As a spy, she was out of practice. "I'm fine, I was just cleaning up some of these files."

His hand slipped to hers and he grasped her fingers. "You're trembling."

When TJ attempted to pull her hand free, Gordon held tighter. "What's wrong? Did I scare you?" He reached for her other hand. "I'm sorry. I didn't mean to." He stared down into her eyes, his face softening. Gordon had always had a thing for TJ and had asked her out on more occasions than she cared to remember.

Tonight, she could smell the alcohol on his breath and she wondered if the added stimulus would make him do or say something stupid. "Are you working late, too?" she asked, hoping he would take the professional track.

"No. I stopped by to pick up a file I needed for the meeting I'll attend first thing in the morning. What about you?"

Her heart thumping against her rib cage, TJ nodded. "I have a report to work on for Congressman Crane." That lie was easier than the lie she'd told the security guard earlier. TJ tugged hard enough to free her hands and stepped away.

"Anything I can help you with?" Gordon closed the distance again.

"No, I can manage on my own. You go home, and get some rest. I'll see you tomorrow." TJ held her breath, praying Gordon would do as she suggested. A quick glance at the clock showed she only had a matter of minutes before Sean showed up. She had to get rid of Gordon or their foray into Crane's office would be impossible.

Gordon reached for her again. "TJ, won't you reconsider and let me take you out for dinner, a drink, dancing…anything?"

Before he could clamp his grip on her again, she backed away, putting a good three feet between them. "Don't, Gordon." TJ hated when he did this. Gordon's dauntless pursuit only made her stomach knot. She didn't love him. Couldn't he take no for an answer? She shook her head. "Much as I like you, Gordon, there's nothing there besides friendship. Please, let's stay friends."

His hands fell to his sides and he nodded. "Okay. Although I wish it were otherwise, you're right. If there's nothing there, there's nothing there. If you're sure you don't need me, I'll head home."

"I don't need you," she said, her tone slow and deliberate, followed by a small smile, nothing big or insincere. "Good night, Gordon."

"Good night, TJ." He left the room, his shoulders slumped and his feet dragging.

After the door closed behind him, TJ let out the breath she'd held and spun back to the files that hung open, a guilty reminder she'd been snooping. Hopefully Gordon wouldn't think anything of her being in Haddock's files late at night.

The door opened again.

Damn! Couldn't he just leave her alone?

TJ spun. The sharp remark poised on her lips died as soon as she saw who it was. "Oh, it's you."

Sean McNeal stood in the doorway, his black polo shirt stretched taut over his muscular chest, accentuating his coal-black hair and striking green eyes. "Expecting someone else?"

Every bone in TJ's body turned to mush. "No, no." Her hands fumbled with the file she'd been holding and she almost dropped it. *Get a grip. It's just Sean.* "I must be punchy from our earlier activities." Instead of the near-death situation on the jogging trail, an image of their embrace sprang to her mind and her face flamed.

"Discover anything?" Sean asked, a smile curling the edges of his lips, a devilish twinkle in his eyes.

TJ's cheeks heated. "Maybe." She handed him the letter and stepped away, out of proximity of his body and the spicy scent of his aftershave.

When Sean finally looked up, TJ was back in control, tenuous though it was. "Do you think that little bit of Millennium Challenge money was enough to get a congressman killed?"

Sean shrugged. "People have been killed for less than that. But the promise of oil has more possibilities. Want to check out Crane's office since he's involved in the Arobo MC proposal?"

"Yes." She needed to move, get out of the office and back on the case. "But we need to wait until the night security guard makes his pass. I don't want to be in Crane's office until after that."

Ten minutes later a hulking young man dressed in the Capitol Police uniform ducked through the door. "Hello, Ms. Barton."

"Hi, Joe."

He glanced from her to Sean. "Evening, Mr. Newman." The six-foot-six mountain of a man hesitated for a moment. "If you two need anything, be sure to yell."

"Thanks, Joe." TJ smiled. "We will."

As the guard left the office, TJ released a long breath. "Give him a few minutes to make it down the hallway and we can go."

They stood in silence for the longest two minutes of TJ's life. Enough time to get her blood rushing through her system at an alarming rate.

Finally, Sean moved to the hall door, glanced out and back to her. "Coast is clear."

Following Sean through the doorway, TJ stumbled, the enormity of what she was doing hitting her at knee level.

"Something wrong?" Sean looked back at her from the hall.

"Yeah, I'm about to aid and abet a possible terrorist. I could lose my career over this without hope of ever getting another job in my lifetime." She laughed. "Other than that, I'm good."

Sean stared long and hard at her. "You don't have to do this for me, you know."

"Get this clear," she said. "I'm not doing this for you. I'm doing this for all those who died in Dindi."

SEAN CAST A QUICK LOOK up and down the hall before stopping in front of Crane's office. "Let's do this."

TJ's hand shook as she inserted her key in the outer office door and paused. "I can get us into the outer office, but Crane always locks his personal office, and he's the only one with the key."

"Just get me out of the hall and I'll do the rest." The door opened, no problem, and Sean pushed through, stopping just inside the doorway. "Not you."

"What do you mean, not me?"

"If I get caught, it should only be on my back, not yours."

"Bull. It's my key that got you this far. All they have to do is read the scanner reports. Now move before someone sees me standing here arguing with you."

TJ hustled into the room, shutting and locking the door behind her.

Sean muttered beneath his breath. "I hate it when you're right."

"Hate is a good thing," she whispered.

He stood for a moment allowing time for his eyes to adjust to the little bit of light shining beneath the door from the hallway. "Where does Crane keep his files?"

"If Congressman Crane had anything to hide, he'd keep it locked in his office."

"Then that's where we'll start." He stepped forward but a hand shot out to grab his arm.

"How to you propose to get in without the key?" TJ asked.

Sean slipped a hard plastic file out of his back pocket and held it up. "Gets past metal detectors every time."

"Yeah, but does it do the job?"

Sean pulled a penlight from his shirt pocket and worked his way through the maze of offices to Crane's door. There, he knelt in front of the knob, inserting the plastic file into the keyhole.

With TJ behind him, her foot tapping a staccato on the carpeted floor, he had difficulty concentrating on his task. After several attempts, he sat back, telling himself it was just a breather. He'd get this door open, in time. Question was, how much time did they have?

"We need to hurry." TJ held out her hand. "We don't have all night."

"You think you can do better?" He shined his light in her face and his heart stuttered at the way her lips twitched as if she were fighting back a smile.

"Let me try." Her hand remained out, palm up, until Sean slapped the file in·it.

Sean stood, his arms crossed over his chest.

TJ knelt beside the door and pressed her ear to the panel. She dug the file into the keyhole and eased it around until an audible click sounded. Her face broke out into a grin and she jumped to her feet. The door swung open to a dark office.

Aware that they had to get in and get out before the security guard came back for his second round, Sean ushered TJ through the door, then locked it behind them.

When she reached out to flip on the light, his hand closed over hers and he squeezed her fingers. "His office has a window to the outside. I'd rather not announce to the public we're in here."

"I knew that." The glow from his penlight accentuated her reddened cheeks. She tugged her hand loose and dug in her pocket. Pulling out a mini flashlight, she shot him a grin. "I came prepared."

The way her eyes lit up hit him in the midsection. TJ might have been prepared for the dark, but Sean wasn't prepared to be only inches away from her in that dark.

When her gaze met his, some of his hunger must have shown in his expression, because her eyes dilated and her lips parted.

He reached out and grabbed her arms.

"What?" TJ stared up at him, her eyes wide.

He wanted to kiss her so badly he could almost taste her lips. For a long moment he hesitated, and then his hands dropped to his sides and he worked his way around the room. "We don't have much time."

A frown furrowed her brow and she chewed her lower lip. Finally she nodded and flicked the switch on her flashlight. "Okay, let's get to work."

As she sifted through the file cabinets lining Congressman Crane's office, TJ fought back her desire to pummel Sean's chest. From hot to cold in a manner of seconds was the only way to describe his actions. He'd wanted to kiss her. TJ could see it in his eyes, feel it in his touch. But he was right. They had to get in and out quickly or risk being caught.

While she dug through the files, Sean picked the lock on Crane's desk.

"See? I can do it. You just had me rattled." His muttered comment made TJ smile.

Was that it? She rattled him? Made him lose his focus and self-control? A surge of feminine power rushed through her. Sean McNeal, the professional agent, admitting to losing focus.

Good. Maybe she'd shake him up a little more once they were out of this office.

TJ registered the squeaking sound of a door hinge in the outer office. Her thoughts crystallized and she panned the room for the nearest place to hide—a closet on the opposite side of the spacious room. She shoved the files she'd been searching back into the cabinets and ran to Crane's office door.

Two voices drifted toward her from the reception area.

Heart pounding, TJ turned to Sean. "Quick, the closet." She raced across the room and jerked open the closet door.

Sean laid the folders he'd been viewing back in the drawers carefully and then leaped for the door TJ held open, clicking his flashlight off as soon as the door closed behind them.

The closet was barely large enough to hold the four suit jackets, a black umbrella and two pairs of dress shoes, much less two grown adults. TJ could only hope whoever came into the office didn't plan on hanging a coat or staying long. With her shoulder pressed into Sean's chest and their recent near-kiss, she knew her willpower would dwindle to nonexistent within a matter of a few pathetic minutes.

Already, the woodsy scent of his cologne had her senses reeling. The heat of his body fitted against her as tightly as a wet suit, made her blood flame. She trembled, the movement shaking her from her shoulders all the way to her wobbly knees.

His lips pressed to her temple and he whispered, "Shhh. It'll be okay."

What did he know? He was turning her inside out without even trying. TJ wanted to elbow him in the gut for making her body crazy with need, but she resisted, knowing any movement might give them away. And how would she explain to one of the congressmen she worked for why she was hiding in his closet? She'd be fired on the spot with charges brought against her for breaking and entering.

Her career swam before her eyes. Before she'd met Sean, if anyone had asked her whether or not she liked her job, she'd have answered with a resounding yes. But now, after sleuthing at St. Croix Financial Services, being chased by a hired killer, and trapped in a closet with the chance of losing her job, TJ wasn't sure she'd regret losing it.

Instead, her blood never sang so sweetly through her veins. Adrenaline surged through her system, setting her nerves on edge and her muscles tensed for action. She felt more alive now than any time since she left the Bureau.

The voices grew louder outside Congressman Crane's office and a thump against his door made TJ jump.

She'd give anything to be able to see what was going on. She could only guess what was happening, with just the sounds to go by.

The member's office door slammed against the wall and a couple pairs of footsteps stumbled across the floor, groans and grunts accompanying the people into the room.

TJ squeezed Sean's hand to keep herself from reaching out for the door handle. Her imagination ran wild over what could be going on out there. Was someone dragging a body in? How would they get past the guards with a body?

The office door slammed shut and a giggle reached TJ's ears, like a woman playing. The giggle was followed by Congressman Crane's voice saying, "Here, let me undo that for you."

Her shoulders relaxing, TJ almost laughed out loud. All this conspiracy theory made her way too punchy.

Crane had a mistress. By the sounds of papers being knocked from the desk and a paperweight hitting the carpeted floor with a soft whomp, they were going at it.

Who was she? TJ ran a list of staffers through her mind. Was it Mandy Swenson, the new blond intern from Michigan? Or the staff assistant they'd hired to fill in for Monique, who'd been killed in the bombing? Whoever it was liked to moan more than talk.

She'd always known Crane was too familiar with the women, but she'd never actually heard of him making a pass at one. Obviously, the rumor mill hadn't gotten hold of this one yet. She'd have to ask Gordon if he'd heard anything she might have missed. In the meantime, she was stuck inside a closet listening to the private antics of a congressman and his latest lover.

The thought of someone making it in the congressman's office made her squirm and the squirming made her aware of Sean's reaction to the situation. Something rigid pressed against her lower back. And it wasn't a flashlight.

Suddenly, the closet was way too small and incredibly hot. TJ tugged at the collar of her blouse as if it were too tight. It had fit fine when she left her apartment earlier that evening.

Muscular arms curved around hers and work-roughened hands slipped around her waist.

The sounds of the room faded into the background of TJ's heartbeat thrumming against her eardrums. For several long moments she remained unbending, fighting her natural inclination to lean against Sean's strength and be cocooned by his hard body. The battle ended when his hand rose up her arm and cupped her chin, turning her toward him.

With an inaudible sigh, she gave up and melted into his kiss. She swiveled around in his arms until her breasts pressed against his chest, her nipples puckering beneath the thin cotton of her blouse.

Sean's tongue pushed past her teeth and in to claim her tongue, twisting and stroking, his touch gentle and possessive.

When TJ finally broke away to breathe, her knees refused to hold her. If not for the strength of Sean's arms, she would have had to lean against the wall to keep from dropping to the floor.

"What's that?" A husky female voice called out on the other side of the wooden door.

TJ's bones stiffened and she jerked upright. Had they been found out? Would Crane turn them in to the Capitol Police? Reminding herself to breathe, TJ straightened her hair and clothing, prepared to face the congressman and his mistress.

"It's the guard making his rounds," Crane said. "We'd better take this to our usual place."

"Of course. You're right." No longer garbled with

grunts and groans, the professional voice of the woman registered loud and clear in TJ's mind. She knew that voice. But it couldn't be. No way. There had to be some mistake

"Are you ready?" Crane said.

"As soon as I zip my dress." She paused and then said, "There. How do I look?"

"Good enough to eat." The representative actually growled.

"Save it, Congressman," she said, her voice laced with a sexy, teasing quality. "For later."

TJ's stomach turned, sick at the thought of what the two had obviously been getting away with for some time.

The sound of a lock being turned on the office door was followed by Congressman Crane's voice. "Hello, Joe."

"Good evening, sir," the security guard responded. "I saw the lights and figured someone was in here. Is it just you two?"

"That's right, but not for long." Crane used the deep voice he used when he spoke publicly. "We have another engagement to attend, so we won't be staying."

"Well, you have a good evening, sir, ma'am." Joe's voice rumbled from the other room.

"We will," the woman responded. "We will."

TJ had to know for certain. She eased open the closet door enough to where she could see Crane and a dark-haired woman standing in the office door.

Crane turned to the woman next to him. "That was close."

"Too close." She leaned toward him and he pulled her into his arms, kissing her soundly. "That's what makes it fun."

"You're a wicked woman."

"And you like it that way, don't you?" Her hand curved around his jawline, and she rose up on her toes to suck on his bottom lip.

"Ummm, yes." He kissed her again, his hand cupping her butt, wrinkling her expensive black dress. Then he backed away and stared at her. "By the way, what was with you telling the Appropriations Committee you didn't support the Arobo MC funding? I thought we agreed on it before the meeting."

She touched his chin with her fingertip. "That's to throw the rest of them off. Can't have everyone thinking I'm your yes-woman, now can I? You have to convince me and them, in public. You know I think Arobo is an excellent candidate for the funding." She paused. "Now, are we going to argue or leave?"

"Makes sense. Let's go. I want you all to myself."

"You go ahead. I have to take care of a little business." She touched her finger to his lips. "I'll only be a few minutes extra."

"Don't take too long. I'll be waiting." He pressed a brief kiss to her fingertips and then flipped the light switch, throwing the room into darkness.

The couple left the office, closing the door and locking it behind them.

TJ, her stomach flipping over in a wash of bile, pushed out of the closet.

Sean's hand snagged her arm before she'd taken two steps. "Be careful, TJ. They might come back."

She moved out into the room, anticipating the slightest sound. "I can't believe we saw what we just saw."

"Me either." Sean stepped lightly across the floor and pressed his ear to the office door. "I don't hear anything."

TJ shook her head in the dark. "Who'd have thought Congressman Crane was having a love affair with Congresswoman Malone?"

Chapter Ten

"I can't believe they're having an affair." As soon as Crane and Malone had left the outer offices, TJ went back to the file cabinet as if driven to find the dirt on Crane. "I know Crane's wife. She's a nice lady."

"Happens when you work closely with someone." He didn't mean to downplay the significance of what they'd witnessed, but the love affair wasn't the reason they were in Crane's office.

"Yeah, but it's not right," TJ muttered.

"How long have you worked around politicians?" Sean asked, sliding the desk drawer open and shining his flashlight at the file he'd laid inside.

"I know, I know." She stared across the room at him, her frown visible in the tiny glow of her mini flashlight. "How will I be able to face them tomorrow?" She looked down at the files in her hands. "Damn."

"Don't take it so hard. Everyone has their weaknesses."

"No, I mean damn, I found something." She held up two folders.

"What are those?"

"Folders with the Arobo Millennium Challenge application in them." She flipped them open and thumbed through the contents.

"So? I thought that was public knowledge."

"Then why does he have two folders, one marked Arobo Millennium Challenge and the other marked Special Project?"

"Arobo might be his special project?"

"Then why would he have documents from Troy Oil Enterprises in the Special Project folder and not in the Arobo folder? The Troy Oil documents detail information about the Arobo offshore oil potential. It's all here, geological sample reports and all."

Sean replaced the papers he'd been working through in the desk and joined her at the files. "Where did you find these?"

"The Arobo folder was filed where I expected it to be under the As. The Special Project folder was in the bottom drawer marked Miscellaneous. It was in a file that looked more like trash."

"This might be something worth looking into. Shine your flashlight on the pages." Sean removed his cell phone from the case on his belt and snapped pictures of the oil exploration documents, one by one, until he'd saved images of the entire report.

As he snapped the last picture, a noise caught Sean's attention and he stared across the folder at TJ. "Did you hear that?"

She nodded, her eyes wide in the glow from her flashlight.

Crane's voice could be heard in the outer office. "I'll just be a minute. I left my brief on my desk."

Sean slammed the folder shut and handed TJ the file.

She placed it in the cabinet and slid the drawer shut as quickly and quietly as she could.

A key in the door clicked the lock open as TJ and Sean dove into the closet for the second time that evening and shut the door behind them.

With his heart pounding in his chest, Sean pulled TJ back into his arms and held her tight. She wrapped her arms around her midsection, her breathing short, shallow puffs.

Sean inhaled the tang of spring flowers, that special TJ scent he'd never forget.

As Crane moved around his office, Sean's hands moved around TJ, touching places he hadn't been since Dindi. TJ's hand closed over his with just enough pressure to encourage rather than discourage his advances.

When the door to the office finally closed behind Crane, Sean didn't move. He wanted to freeze the moment and the closeness he shared with TJ. "What are we going to do?"

"About the Arobo file?" she asked, her voice soft and breathy as she leaned her back against his chest, and brought his hands to her breasts.

"No, about us." His fingers brushed over her nipples, her turgid peaks thrusting out against the flimsy material of her blouse and lacy bra.

She turned in his arms and reached up to cup his face in her hands. Then, standing on her tiptoes, she pressed her lips to his.

Denying his attraction to this woman was a losing battle. He captured her face between his hands and kissed her. Tomorrow seemed soon enough to face the consequences.

TJ's arms crept around his waist and she pulled him close. When they broke apart, she leaned her forehead against his chest. "You're making me crazy, Sean."

"Same here." He kissed the top of her head. "We need to get out of here before Joe comes looking for us."

"I know." For several more seconds she didn't move in the darkness and then she sighed and pushed away. "I guess you'll be running the photos by the agency?"

"Yeah, after I take you home." Sean smoothed his thumbs across her cheekbones and down to trace her lips. He wished he could see her expression. "Do you want me to stop by after?"

"No." Her response was quick and she pressed a kiss to his thumb. "Ah, hell, who am I kidding? Would you?"

A SHIVER OF ANTICIPATION feathered across TJ's skin and she counted ten of the longest minutes of her life before she closed and locked Haddock's door and left. Sean had left well ahead of her, and was waiting in the parking garage.

TJ made the trek across the Rayburn Building into the Longworth Building in record time, waving at the guards as she breezed out into the garage.

Wow, was she really going to meet with Sean on her turf? In her tiny apartment? And for what? The possibilities made her absolutely giddy.

They didn't talk much on the ride to her apartment. After arriving Sean searched it for intruders.

"I could have done that," she insisted.

"And if you'd found someone?"

"I was trained—"

"In self-defense. I know." Standing in front of the

door, he stared down at her. "These people mean serious business."

A chill slithered down her back at the memory of the carnage in Dindi. "You don't have to tell me that."

"You know the drill. Don't let anyone in and don't leave. I'll be back in twenty minutes." He brushed a kiss across her lips and left.

TJ stared at the door for several long seconds.

A hard knock made her jump. "Lock the door."

Flustered that he'd caught her falling down on the job, she shoved the bolt home and stood back, embarrassment and distance clearing her head of Sean. She should've told him not to come back, she didn't need him.

In an effort to use some energy, she threw in a load of laundry and stacked the dishwasher. Both tasks required little thought, but ate up the time.

She wanted to know who'd bombed the embassy as much as Sean did. That's why, deep down, she supposed she trusted him.

Dishes done, a load of laundry swirling away in the washer and she still hadn't burned up the energy generated by the kiss in Crane's closet.

She marched to her bedroom and looked for something to clean. Just as she bent to straighten the shoes in her closet, the lights blinked out.

TJ dropped to a crouch, her heart slamming against her ribs. How long had it been since Sean left? Ten minutes, fifteen max.

The skies had been clear, no thunderstorms in the area. Then why had the electricity gone off?

Her answer came with a loud crash that could only be the picture window breaking in the living room.

Fumbling around in the dark, TJ searched for a weapon, anything to protect herself. She had a 9 mm pistol in her nightstand on the opposite side of the room.

TJ scrambled around the bed, banging her leg against the bedpost. Just as she reached into the drawer for the gun, a hand clamped over her mouth at the same time a tree trunk of an arm circled her waist, trapping one of her arms. The acrid stench of body odor gagged her and the arm around her belly tightened.

TJ's heart leapt in her chest and she dropped low, her self-defense training kicking in. *Don't let him get you off your feet.* While she bit into his hand, she used her free arm to slam an elbow into his gut.

The man grunted, but didn't let go of her body. He did let go of her mouth long enough to whack the side of her head with his injured hand.

Before she could let out more than a squeak, the hand covered her mouth again.

Again she dug her elbow into his side and, at the same time, pounded her heel into the top of his foot.

Her attacker cursed and loosened his hold around her middle enough that TJ ducked beneath his arm, pushed him from behind and ran for the door.

Fingers clutched at her blazer, yanking her backward.

TJ shrugged out of the jacket. She flung the decorative end table to the floor behind her and raced to the door. With the sound of her attacker stumbling over furniture at her heels, she managed to unlock the door in record time, fling it open and race down the steps.

Running as fast as her sturdy pumps could carry her, she figured her best bet was to outrun him to the nearest well-lit all-night convenience store. She knew of one two blocks away. Elbows pumping and heart pounding, TJ rounded the overgrown hedge at the corner of the building and ran into a solid wall of muscle. The impact knocked the air from her lungs.

Recovering quickly, she brought her hands up and slammed her fist into the second guy's gut. If her chances of getting away from one man were slim, two would border on impossible. But if they wanted her badly enough, there'd be hell to pay and she'd be the devil.

Rough hands grabbed her arms and held her away. "TJ, what the hell?" Sean's voice cut through the force of her survival instinct and she stopped kicking, but not before she landed a hard heel to his right shin.

"Damn!" He turned his face skyward and muttered more curses under his breath, his hands tightening on her arms. Then he looked down at her. "Mind telling me what all that was about?"

His hands loosened and TJ spun in the direction she'd come, bracing herself for the man who'd attacked her. "Didn't you see him?"

"See who?"

"The man who attacked me."

Sean shoved her behind him. "Where?"

"In my apartment."

Sean turned to her. "Stay here."

"Are you crazy? I'm going with you. We don't know if the guy's armed. You might get hurt."

"On second thought, maybe you should come with me. I can't leave you standing out here alone." When she moved up beside him, he shot a narrow-eyed look at her. "Stay behind me."

"Why?"

"Just do it."

Stubborn man. TJ would have argued more, but the bad guy might still be around the corner. "Okay, okay. But I'm a big girl. I can handle him as well as you can."

As Sean jogged toward the corner of the building, TJ hurried to keep up.

Sean pulled a knife from his pocket and clicked it open, the steely blade catching the light from the street-lamp. Then he ducked low and peered around the bush.

Adrenaline pulsing through her, TJ willed herself to stay calm.

Sean hovered for several seconds before he disappeared into the shadows near her apartment door.

Panic threatened to set in and TJ followed, determined to keep him in sight. Hugging the shadows, she crept around the bush where Sean had been.

He wasn't there. How had he moved so fast? And where did he go? Had he gone into the apartment?

As she stared at the darkened door, she couldn't breathe. Images of the bombed-out building in Dindi slammed through her mind. How dare he go in there without her? How dare he leave her again?

Anger surged and she left the safety of the bushes, charging toward the open door. If he wasn't dead already, she'd kill him for making her worry.

An engine roared to life a block away and headlights shot a pattern of light away from her.

Sean leaped through the apartment door and took off after the taillights, only to stop after twenty yards. The car had disappeared around the corner and no amount of racing on foot would catch it.

"Get a tag number?" she asked.

"No." Sean grabbed her hand and pulled her back into the apartment, shutting the door behind them.

The anger still prominent and roiling, TJ trembled and strained to see Sean in the darkness.

Sean slipped an arm around her waist and steered her down the hallway to the kitchen. "Do you have a flashlight or candle?"

"In the cabinet over the stove."

When he'd located a flashlight, he tromped back to where she'd stopped in the living room and shone the light in her face, a fierce frown pushing his brows together. "Did he hurt you?"

TJ shook her head and dragged in a deep breath. She stood in her living room with shattered glass flung across the carpet and furniture and the dam broke. Now that the danger was over, the emotions she'd held at bay bombarded her with the force of a flash flood. "No, he didn't hurt me, no thanks to you. And don't ever go off and leave me standing outside a building ever again. Do you understand me?" She pushed her hands against his chest. "Don't ever do it again."

"What are you talking about?" Sean stepped back, his forehead creasing. "Are you mad about something?"

"Damn right I'm mad."

"For coming to your rescue?"

"My rescue?" She spun away from him and stomped across broken glass. "Of all the pigheaded, chauvinistic things to say." She marched back to him until she stood toe-to-toe. "For the record, I can rescue myself, thank you very much." She poked his chest with her finger. "I don't need some undercover agent to come running when I get in a bind. Especially one who plays dead for a month and expects me to fall right back into his life as if he never died." She poked her finger in his chest again, her cheeks flaming red. "You're damn right I'm mad. I've broken into a congressman's office and allowed you to photograph confidential documents. I don't even know if you're one of the good guys." She flung her arm in the air. "Just who the hell do you work for? Tell me that."

"I can't."

She continued as if he hadn't said anything. "I thought you were a safe businessman. Someone I could count on not getting hurt in a firefight. You let me think you died in that bombing. You left me standing outside my apartment wondering if the bad guy was in there ready to blow you away all over again."

"TJ." He reached out to grab her arms, but she shook him off.

"Don't touch me. In fact, get out of my apartment." She stomped to the door and jerked it open. "Just go." Tears trembled on her lashes, one edged over the top, spilling down her cheek.

Sean finally saw through her blustery tirade. All her anger boiled down to one thing—TJ had been afraid for him. As he strode toward her, Sean's heart melted. "I'm sorry." Instead of leaving as she demanded, he pulled her hand loose and closed the door, shutting them in and the world out. "I'm sorry."

Then she was in his arms, her face pressed to his chest, her shoulders shaking with silent sobs. Her fist clenched and she made a pathetic attempt at beating it against his chest. "You died once. Don't let it happen again."

"You're right. I'm a jerk for letting you think I was dead."

"Yes…" She sniffed and looked up at him. "You're a jerk."

"And I'll be forever in the doghouse for that one itty-bitty set of lies, won't I?" He brushed a tear off her cheek with his finger. "Just don't cry, TJ. It makes your eyes puffy."

"Oh, you!" She pushed against his chest.

Refusing to let her out of his arms, Sean held tight. TJ hiccupped and sniffed. "Let me go."

He hated it when she cried and he felt like a heel for being the reason, but he couldn't resist teasing. "You're ex-FBI. If you really wanted out of this situation, you'd figure out a way."

"Don't think I won't." Her trembling lip stiffened and her brows drew together in a determined frown.

"I'm counting on it, because *I* can't seem to leave." Then he gave in to his desire and claimed her lips. The salty taste of her tears made him delve deeper. His arms swept around her and pulled her close.

When TJ reached for the buttons on his shirt, he clasped her hands and held them against his chest. "Much as I'd like to, we shouldn't."

TJ OPENED HER EYES to sunlight streaming through a crack in the blinds. After a quick glance at her alarm, she sat up straight in bed. Seven-thirty? Yikes! She had to be at work in thirty minutes. Why the hell hadn't her alarm woken her?

The pillow beside her was creased, but the comforter covered the side of the bed where Sean had slept. Disappointment battled with reason that he hadn't made love to her, but she knew he'd made the right decision.

After all that had happened and with so much still up in the air, they would have been fools to make love. Sean had opted for holding her until she finally went to sleep.

TJ sat up and rubbed the sleep from her eyes.

When had Sean left? And why hadn't he woken her to tell her he was leaving or kiss her goodbye before going to the office?

What did she expect? Sean had a job to do and so did she. Hadn't he said distraction could get a person killed?

But he'd left without telling her.

"Shoot! I preferred it when boys still had cooties." She flung the sheets aside and stomped to the bathroom. Thirty minutes was barely enough time to get ready and get to work. She certainly didn't have time to ruminate on her on-again-off-again relationship with Sean McNeal.

TJ showered and dressed in less than fifteen minutes. She combed her wet hair back into a slick ponytail, applied a minimal amount of makeup and slipped into the standard black business suit jacket and trousers with a plain white cotton blouse.

She had some questions she wanted to ask of Congressman Crane before the office got too busy or he was called off to one of the multitude of committee meetings scheduled throughout the day. Although how she could face him and not envision Congresswoman Malone all over him last night might be a problem.

Well, she'd just have to deal with it. She wasn't sure she wanted to blow the whistle and ruin two members' careers over a little hanky-panky. It fried her goat that they were conducting their affair in government offices, paid for by the taxpayers.

When TJ entered Crane's outer office, she spotted Gordon Harris speaking to one of Crane's assistants and headed straight for him. "Good morning, Gordon."

"Hi, TJ." He looked up and smiled. "Looks like you just got out of the shower. Is this a new look for you?"

"Not hardly. My alarm didn't go off this morning and I didn't have time to dry my hair." Her body warmed at the real reason. "Is Congressman Crane in his office?" she asked his assistant.

The woman nodded. "Yes, ma'am."

"Could I speak to him next?"

The assistant glanced at her computer. "He's got an appointment in five minutes."

"I won't take long."

The assistant shrugged. "He should be out in a minute."

TJ pulled Gordon to the side, out of earshot from the assistant. "Gordon, what more do you know about the Arobo MC funding?"

"Not much more than you do. Crane is handling that one on his own. He hasn't involved his assistants from what I've heard." Gordon frowned and tapped a pen on the desk. "You're the second person who's asked me about Arobo this morning. What's the big deal?"

"Second?"

Gordon glanced at his watch. "I'm late for a meeting. Can we talk about this later?"

"Sure." Even as she said the word, the door opened.

Sean McNeal stepped out, his hand closed around the file marked Arobo. While TJ slept in, Sean had been at work.

TJ's gaze met his and a thrill of awareness tingled throughout her body, reminding her that last night hadn't been a dream. No dream could be as memorable as their kiss and how he'd held her until she'd fallen to sleep.

She nodded as he walked by.

TJ knew she should keep out of the investigation. It was Sean's job, not hers. But her life had been threatened more than once. She'd be damned if she'd sit back and do nothing.

Before Crane could grab his coat to leave, she stepped into his office. "Sir, do you have a moment?"

"I'm on my way to the Budget Committee meeting. You can walk with me if you like."

"Yes, sir."

He lifted his jacket from the coatrack in the corner, shoved his arms into the sleeves and turned. "What is it you need?"

After a deep breath, TJ launched into the lie she'd practiced on the way over from her apartment, hoping she wasn't walking all over whatever Sean had done previously. "Sir, I'm working with Congresswoman Malone on drafting a status letter to the Dindi National Government concerning the MC funding." She held her breath and waited for his response, knowing for a fact the letter had already been drafted two days prior. She was banking on Crane not being aware of that little detail.

"Malone's sure been busy this morning." He grunted. "Good. It's about time she saw it my way. Now why can't you get that information from Grant Futrell? As Haddock's former chief of staff, he should have that data."

"He took off for another meeting. Since you're in charge of the Arobo MC funding, I thought you could help me word the status report. How should I tell Dindi they will be refused the funding when the Arobo funding appears to be a go?"

Crane shot a narrow-eyed look at her. "Who said Arobo was a go?"

She forced her lips to turn up in a smile when all she wanted was to shake the information out of him. "Scuttlebutt has that it's a done deal."

"Scuttlebutt isn't always accurate and I'm surprised you would adhere to it. The committee could turn down the proposal for Arobo at any time and approve Dindi."

"Very true. However, if Arobo is approved, the letter needs sufficient meat to appease the Dindi government for losing the funding."

"Basically, the Dindi government doesn't show sufficient control over its population to ensure the safety of foreign nationals interested in developing the country's natural resources." As they traversed the hallway, Crane's strides grew longer.

Her legs a good six inches shorter, TJ all but ran to keep up. "Didn't Arobo have an uprising not eighteen months ago? If they get funding and Dindi doesn't, won't that look suspicious?"

Crane stopped so fast, TJ almost ran into him. "Ms. Barton, I don't have time for this discussion. See your chief of staff."

Nothing like angering a congressman to further crater your career. TJ couldn't believe her own tenacity. As Crane turned to leave, TJ asked one more question. "Sir, I'm curious. Why are you handling this *special project* all by yourself instead of letting one of your staff do it?"

His body stiffened and he pivoted on one heel to face

her. Red pigment rose from beneath his Armani suit collar, suffusing his cheeks with ruddy splotches before his lips formed words. "Young lady, I suggest you stick to your own projects."

Maybe it was one of her gut instincts, but she gambled and took the plunge. "Sir, I'm just concerned over the rumors I'm hearing."

"You obviously have too much idle time since Haddock's death. I'll speak with your chief of staff. Good day." This time he walked away.

If she was going to sabotage her career, she might as well do it in a big way. "Sir, the rumors have it the bombing wasn't just a random act of terrorism. Some say it was all about which country would receive the money."

Crane had taken five steps when her words hit him. He spun and marched back to where she stood in the hallway, his face flaming red. Standing nearly nose to nose, Crane said in a low, menacing voice, "Making a statement like that in a public place can land you in a legal battle so deep you won't be able to dig your way out. I suggest you watch your tongue and stop spreading unfounded rumors. The bombing was a random act of terrorism against the United States. Nothing more, nothing less. Do I make myself clear?"

"Crystal, sir." *You pompous, adulterous jerk.* "And the MC proposal for Arobo has nothing to do with lobbyist Jason Frazier or Troy Oil Enterprises. It's all perfectly clear to me. Have a good day, Congressman Crane." This time, TJ turned and walked away. When she reached a corner, she risked a glance back.

Congressman Crane still stood where she'd left him, his brows drawn in a severe frown. People passing him in the hallway steered clear of him and his ferocious look.

Congresswoman Malone stepped out of an office to his right and joined him in the hallway. With their heads bent together, they spoke in hushed tones, each darting a glance her way.

TJ turned her back and walked away. Had Crane orchestrated the bombing in Dindi? If so, he'd be running scared about now.

Her eyes narrowed. Was he the one who'd sicked a thug on her to keep her quiet? Would her persistence make him that much more determined to squelch her dogged pursuit?

Chapter Eleven

Without knocking, Sean marched into Royce's office at noon.

Royce tapped a hand to the earpiece looped around his ear, indicating he was in the middle of a call. He jerked his head toward a chair.

Ignoring his unspoken suggestion to take a seat, Sean paced in front of his boss's desk.

"Good job, Tazer. If you'll fax that list, we'll look into it." Royce pressed a button on the cell phone clipped to his waist, stood and stretched. "Valdez said TJ got to work all right this morning."

"Thanks for sending him over to follow her." Sean had called in for backup that morning. He hadn't liked leaving TJ alone at her apartment or on the city streets when he'd gone to work. With one of the S.O.S. agents guarding her, he could continue on his mission to learn more about what was going on in the Rayburn Building. He felt no closer to finding the person responsible for funding the Dindi bombing, and now TJ was in danger. Something had to give.

As expected, Royce's brows dipped and he shot a

narrow, piercing look at Sean. "Anything besides the attack happen last night that you'd like to tell me about?" That all-knowing look continued as if urging Sean to spill his guts.

Sean wasn't ready to tell Royce about his night in TJ's apartment. There wasn't anything else to say. Other than the one scorching kiss, he'd held her in his arms all night. One of the hardest nights of his life. "We checked out Congressman Crane's office last night and found a few interesting things."

Royce came around the large wooden desk to stand near Sean. "Such as?"

Sean handed printed copies of the reports he'd photographed with his cell phone. "Oil exploration reports from a company called Troy Oil. It appears there's a fairly substantial oil reserve off the coast of Arobo, Dindi's neighbor and rival." Sean filled him in on where they'd found it and the duplicate files being kept in Crane's office. "While we were in his office, Crane walked in."

Royce's his eyes widened. "That's lousy luck. What did he say?"

"TJ and I managed to hide in a closet." His memory of the dark closet was still vibrant in his mind. "Crane had a female guest with him and there was some heavy petting going on."

Royce's brows rose high on his forehead. "Say again?"

Sean shook his head. "Crane had Congresswoman Malone with him and they weren't discussing the government."

Royce's mouth dropped open. "No kidding? The tough-as-nails congresswoman everyone has pegged as our first female presidential candidate?"

Sean nodded, still stunned by what he'd seen.

Royce ran a hand through his short, graying hair. "Wow. Hard to believe they'd risk their careers."

"Yeah. Makes me wonder though, whether or not Malone's involved in the Arobo proposal as well as Crane. It doesn't make sense."

"No it doesn't."

"Any leads on the canoe?"

"As a matter of fact, Tazer just found the canoe rental. The Elite Rowing Club—a very exclusive club, not open to the public. Invitation only. She got a list of those who checked in a canoe late yesterday evening and of those canoes that didn't."

Tim Trainer poked his head in the door. "So were you expecting a fax?" He held up one of the two sheets of paper in his hand.

"Yes, thanks, Tim." Royce held out his hand.

Tim joined them in the office, handing the first sheet to Royce.

Sean leaned over his shoulder and scanned the list of names, most of which he recognized, like a Who's Who of Washington, D.C. As he reached the bottom, he almost missed the second to the last name. Jason Frazier.

Sean shook his head. "What the hell was Jason Frazier doing with Eddy Smith?"

Tim raised the other sheet of paper he still held. "I can answer that one. I ran a scan on large sums of money deposited to the St. Croix Financial Services account in the past six months. Two, in particular, stood out, both for two hundred and fifty thousand dollars each. One of the deposits was made prior to the bombing, the other, after. I traced the source back to T.O. Enterprises."

"And?" Sean asked.

"I did a little more digging and found this list of T.O. Enterprises stockholders. Seems your man Frazier is one of them." He held the list out to Sean.

Sean scanned the list of stockholders. No other names jumped out except Jason Frazier's.

Tim stepped to the door and waved. "Back to my cave. I'm sure there's more dirt where that came from."

"Good job, Tim," Royce called after him.

When Tim's footsteps faded down the hallway, Sean closed the door. "One other thing."

Royce crossed his arms over his chest. "TJ?"

Sean nodded. "She cornered Congressman Crane and asked some pretty pointed questions about the Arobo Millennium Challenge issue."

"What did he say?"

"He got angry and told her to mind her own business." Sean pressed the bridge of his nose, forcing back a headache growing there. "She's in this too deep."

"Stick to her," Royce advised. "Don't let her leave the Rayburn Building without you."

"She's feisty, independent and makes her own decisions." Not to mention, she'd defended herself admirably the previous evening. She might not always be so lucky. "I'm trying."

"Do the best you can." Royce lifted a file from his desk. "By the way, we have more information on her." The older man stared at the file before tossing it back on his desk. "She quit the FBI six months after her partner was shot and paralyzed by a bullet to the spine."

Was that why she refused to partner with another

agent? Having lost his closest friend, Sean knew how bad it hurt. But to lose a partner to paralysis had to be worse.

"She wasn't there when it happened from the information we were able to glean, so it wasn't her fault. But she quit the Bureau anyway." Royce's gaze pinned Sean's. "Maybe there was something between her and her partner."

A stab of jealousy hit Sean, leaving his gut knotted with the impact. Had TJ been in love with her partner?

"Look, I don't know what's going on between you two, and I'm not sure I want to. But if you get into trouble, you know where I am." Royce slapped a hand on Sean's back.

"Thanks." Sean figured he was already in trouble, but he wasn't so sure Royce could help him out of it.

"In the meantime, I'll put a tail on Jason Frazier. Kat's been after me to get involved in this case. And I'll put Valdez on Eddy Smith."

Sean frowned. "You sure Kat should be involved so soon?"

"She needs to focus on something. She's drifting and I don't know what else will bring her back. Maybe helping find Marty's killer will bring closure."

"Let's hope we find him before he strikes again. This city doesn't need another September eleventh."

TJ GLANCED AT THE WALL clock across from her desk for the tenth time in the past hour. Five-thirty. And she hadn't seen Sean since after her meeting in the hallway with Crane.

He'd been angry that she'd questioned Crane. He didn't want her involved in the case any more than she'd already been. Somehow his fierce whispering seemed more intense than a good loud argument.

"All I need you to do is keep quiet about my identity. Nothing more," he said.

"Are you forgetting I let you into Crane's office? I could be fired and brought up on charges."

"If you're worried about breaking laws, don't. We can offer protection from the government. Just trust me and stay out of this."

"You asked me to trust you. Why should I? You won't even tell me who you work for. I'm supposed to go blindly along with everything you say?" She'd slammed her notebook shut. "No more."

He'd stormed out and hadn't been back since. All day long, TJ stayed close to her office, waiting for the other shoe to drop. But Crane hadn't fired her and Sean hadn't returned.

Her knee bounced beneath the desk—a nervous habit when she was keyed up and strung out on five cups of coffee. With only three hours of sleep the previous night, she'd been snapping at everyone.

"The time doesn't move any faster when you watch the clock." Gordon stepped up to her desk with a stack of documents in his hands. "Are you in a hurry to go somewhere?"

TJ stared at the documents Gordon laid in her in-box. "Not if that stack needs to be dealt with by tomorrow."

"Don't worry. You have a little more lead time on these. Nothing has to be turned in tomorrow."

"Good. I'm beat and I wanted to get home at a reasonable hour tonight."

"Aren't you going to Congressman Crane's cock-

tail party? I understand his place in Foxhall is something to see."

"I don't know. Sounds like it'll be a bunch of boring
politicians patting each other on the back all evening.
I'm just not up to it tonight." She'd rather know where
one undercover agent was.

Ah hell, she just wanted to know where he was for
herself, and if his plans for the evening included her
in any way.

Gordon perched on the edge of the desk, lifted her lead
crystal paperweight and balanced it in his hand. "You've
been crabby all day, did you have a rough night?"

Rough night? TJ slumped back in her chair, too
exhausted to be professional. "You could say that."
Although she wouldn't describe the previous night as
all bad. Dangerous and crazy, but not all bad. There had
been moments…

"Wanna talk about him?" Gordon's gaze lifted from
the paperweight to her eyes.

A flush of heat rose up her throat, giving her away.
"No." Her response was sharper than she'd intended
and she sighed. "There's nothing to talk about. I met a
guy, he's wrong for me, I'm wrong for him. The end."

"Haven't you ever heard the saying 'two wrongs
make a right'?"

TJ rolled her eyes and forced a laugh. "That's not
how it goes. Two wrongs don't make a right."

"Whatever. If two people love each other enough,
they find a way to make it work."

A noise at the door alerted TJ to someone coming in,
and she rose from her desk, her face heating. When she
peered over Gordon's shoulder and saw Sean standing

there, her heart fluttered and her tongued knotted. Had he heard her words?

Gordon turned and smiled his ever-professional smile. "Hello, John. Is there something you need?"

"I had information for TJ. But, if this isn't a good time, I'll come back."

"Not at all, I was just leaving." His hands rose to grip TJ's elbows. "Get some rest, will ya?"

She nodded. "Yes. Thank you, Gordon."

TJ tucked a strand of hair behind her ear and blew out a long breath. *Stick to professional.* "You said you had information?"

"I stopped by the agency and filled them in on last night's attack and your conversation with Crane this morning."

She nodded and waited for him to continue.

"Tazer found out who might have rented that canoe."

"Who?"

"Jason Frazier, your lobbyist from Troy Oil."

"He's not my lobbyist." She hated that her voice sounded defensive. After all that had happened, she deserved to be a little cranky.

"What's the matter? Didn't you get enough sleep last night?"

"You know damn well I didn't," she snapped, her face impossibly hot.

He smiled at her brusque reply. "You might be interested to know, Tim found some rather large deposits in the St. Croix Financial Services account equaling five hundred thousand dollars."

TJ's heart slammed against her chest. Had they found

their killer? "That's the exact amount transferred to the terrorist's account. Who deposited it?"

"Troy Oil."

"So what? They're into stocks and bonds. I'm sure they're used to dealing in large sums."

"Not when they were deposited directly to Trey Masterson's account and that money was transferred to the Caribbean Island account."

"Troy Oil funded the killer. We should be able to call in the police and have them question Jason Frazier."

"Whoa, wait a minute."

"Why? Don't you want to see Marty's killer brought to justice?"

"Since when is everything as it appears on the surface? Think about it."

Her brows knit. "You think there are others involved?"

"Possibly. If we blow the lid on it now, we might not get the others."

"Others being Congressman Crane?" As she said the words, the air left her lungs. "Wow. Do you think Crane is that desperate to get this deal?"

"Maybe, or it could be Frazier's working alone. We don't know. Royce put a tail on Jason Frazier and another on Eddy Smith to see if their movements lead anywhere else. The evidence of Jason's connection to Eddy Smith is pretty damning."

"Why do you suppose Frazier was meeting with Eddy yesterday?"

"Good question." Sean paced across the office floor, staring at his feet as he went. "It has me concerned."

"Do you think Eddy is blackmailing him for more money?"

"Maybe." He looked up at her. "I hope they're not planning another attack."

A chill shook her from head to toe. "Another bombing?"

"Who knows?" Sean dug in his back pocket and pulled out his wallet, extracting a business card with Royce's telephone number on it. "I don't want you leaving this building alone. If I'm not here to escort you, call Royce and he'll send someone."

"I don't need a babysitter or a bodyguard." Part of her thrilled at his concern for her welfare. The other part chafed at his highhandedness. "I handled myself without your help last time. I can do it again."

"Eddy Smith has connections with the mob. Professional killers. If he made a mistake underestimating you, you can be damn sure he won't make that same mistake again." He lifted her hand and turned her palm upward. "Please take the card for me."

His emerald-green eyes, dark with concern, shone down at her and she couldn't pull away. "Okay. But I'm not a wimp."

"No one said you were." He curled her fingers around the card and then pressed his lips to her knuckles. "Thanks."

Maybe not a wimp, but definitely a marshmallow where Sean was concerned. How did the guy do it? He had her mad as hell one moment and eating out of his hand the next. The roller coaster of emotions she'd been on since he'd risen from the dead threatened to derail her.

Sean's cell phone buzzed on his hip and he flipped it open. "What's up, boss?"

By boss, Sean had to mean Royce from the agency.

He'd never be so casual with Congresswoman Malone. TJ leaned closer, anxious to hear the latest.

Sean tensed, his eyes widening. "When?"

TJ's pulse pounded against her ears. What now?

"Any sign of forced entry?" Sean shook his head. "Must have been someone he knew. Is Valdez tailing Eddy? He might decide the heat's on and bolt. He is? Good. I'll be by in a few minutes." He clicked his phone shut and stared across the floor at TJ. "Kat found Jason in his apartment."

TJ fought to breathe. "Dead?"

Sean nodded. "You ready to learn more about the company I work for?"

Chapter Twelve

Royce had called all available agents into the War Room and he'd included TJ. He paced the length of the conference table, a frown creasing his brow. "With Frazier dead, we'll have our work cut out for us to get any evidence on who he was working with."

Valdez tapped a pen to the tabletop. "Why not bring Eddy Smith in for a little questioning?"

"We don't want to spook whoever he's working with," Sean said. "If we bring in Eddy and let him go, he'll warn his boss."

"Possibly blowing our chances to catch him," Tim finished.

"Right." Royce made another pass through the room, head down, brow wrinkled. "We have the financial connection between Frazier and Eddy, but we need to know if anyone else was calling the shots." Royce scratched his chin. "With Crane's association with Jason Frazier, he could have been involved in the Dindi bombing."

"Tazer's following Eddy," Kat noted. "If there's any connection between Eddy and the congressman, she'll know about it."

"*If* Crane's stupid enough to meet with Eddy. We need evidence." Sean stared across at TJ. "And I don't think he'd keep anything in his office."

"He had that secret file," TJ reminded him.

"Yeah." Royce drew the word out. "That doesn't mean he actually gave the order."

"No, but I can't imagine he has any documentation stating it either. Wonder what the scuttlebutt is right now, if they've heard about Jason Frazier's death yet." TJ shot a glance across the table at Sean. "Weren't you invited to Crane's party tonight? It's at his house in Foxhall."

Sean loved the way TJ's brown eyes lit when she was excited with an idea. She'd taken the S.O.S. organization in stride, promising to keep quiet about its existence and the people involved. Instinctively, Sean knew he could trust her. "Maybe we should make an appearance."

"That's what I'm thinking." She glanced at her watch. "Which gives us exactly thirty minutes to get ready. I'd better get going." TJ leaped from her seat and headed for the door.

Sean's heart thudded against his ribs. "Not without an escort."

She faced him, hands on her hips. "I told you, I don't need a bodyguard."

"Yes, you do." He strode across the room and stood directly in front of her. "You're not leaving this building by yourself, and you're not going to your apartment without me or someone I trust."

"Look, buster." She inched closer until they were almost toe to toe and nose to nose. "You're not the boss of me."

If Royce, Kat, Tim and Valdez hadn't been in the room, Sean would have kissed TJ back to her senses.

Kat laughed. "I think you've met your match."

"I like a woman with spirit." Valdez rose from his seat. "I'll stick to her like glue."

Valdez was the Romeo of the group, a real ladies' man. Sean didn't like the idea of him alone with TJ any more than letting her go out on her own.

Royce hooked TJ's elbow in his hand. "I'm headed your way and it would be my pleasure to escort you. It's not as if I'd be playing bodyguard, I'd just be following you in traffic."

Her frown smoothed and she smiled up at Royce. "Only because you said that like a gentleman, I'll take you up on the offer."

Sean's lips pinched together. He didn't like the way Royce had his hand on TJ or smooth-talked her. Not that Royce was like Valdez, but still. "I'll pick you up in thirty minutes. Call me if you hear, see or smell anything suspicious."

"Even if it's the mold growing in my refrigerator?" She hooked her arm through Royce's and treated him to a smile. "Ready?"

Royce smiled. "I don't think anyone is ready for you, TJ."

She shot a defiant look toward Sean. "Damn right." As she strolled through the S.O.S. office door, she called out over her shoulder, "See ya in a few."

Sean stood in the office scratching his head. What was he going to do with her? If he didn't kill her, he'd have to…what?

Kat straightened a stack of papers and stood. "You look like you're not feeling well, Sean. Are you all right?"

"I don't know." He scrubbed his hand down his face and focused on Kat. The circles under her eyes were no less prominent today than they'd been a few days earlier. "I'm fine. How are you holding up?"

"All right, although seeing Jason Frazier with a bullet through his head was unexpected." She shrugged. "Not like I haven't seen homicides before. There were at least a half-dozen a week in the metro area when I was on the force."

"Sometimes I forget you were a D.C. cop." He shook his head and stared at her with even more respect. "That was a big change for a girl from Alaska, huh?"

"I wouldn't call Anchorage small. But compared to D.C…. Yeah, it was a huge adjustment."

"Had to have been rough."

"At times. But you take the risks if you love the job."

"Is that the way you feel about S.O.S.?"

She hesitated, staring toward the window. The sun had dipped below the horizon, with the gray light waning toward darkness. One at a time, the streetlamps flickered on, making the city below bright and cheerful. "Yeah, I guess."

"Still missing Marty, aren't you?"

She sighed and turned to face him. "Yeah. At times I feel like our life together was a dream. We were only married a year and not together for a good portion of it, what with both of us on different jobs at different times. I keep thinking it was all a dream and we never really had that time together."

Sean reached out and lifted her hand. "If you had it all to do again, would you have married Marty?"

She stared up into his eyes, her own filling with tears. "Yes."

He shouldn't ask the next question, but he had to know for himself. "Even knowing you'd lose him?"

"I can't deny it hurts like hell, but I keep thinking about all the good times I'd have missed if I hadn't been with Marty." Tears spilled down her cheeks and onto his hand. "I miss him."

Sean pulled her into his arms and held her. This is what a wife of his would endure if he didn't make it back from a mission. How could he even contemplate putting a woman through this?

Kat pulled away and stared up at Sean, her cheeks still damp, but the tears stopped for the moment. "You need to go."

"You sure you're going to be okay?"

She gave him a crooked grin. "Yeah, I'm an S.O.S. agent. I'm tough." Then she sniffed.

"Yeah, you're tough." Sean leaned down and kissed her forehead. "I need to change. Get some sleep, will you?" His arms dropped from around her and he turned toward the door.

"Hey, Sean?"

"Yeah?" He glanced over his shoulder.

"Don't give up on love because of your job."

Had she taken to reading minds?

Sean turned his back on her. "If I get killed, where would that leave her?" As soon as he said the words, he regretted them and turned to tell Kat so.

She held up her hand, her eyes shimmering with

tears. "If you really love a woman, give her the chance to make that choice herself."

"Who says there's a woman?"

"Like everyone can't tell?" Kat gave a strangled snort. "Go to work, McNeal."

THIRTY MINUTES WERE barely enough to get home in the traffic, much less dress for a congressman's cocktail party.

TJ ran through the apartment kicking off her shoes and stripping down to her underwear, leaving a trail of clothing in her wake.

She rifled through her closet and yanked out a royal-blue strapless dress and weighed its pros and cons. Looked great, but too obvious? Jamming it back in the closet, she reached for a go-to-hell red dress, cut low in the back and high in the front. "What was I thinking when I bought this?" The dress went great with her blond hair, but she was working tonight, not out to catch herself a man. What did any woman wear when she went to a congressman's house to spy on him with a man who made her toes curl when he kissed her?

What did any woman wear when she wasn't sure?

The standard little black dress. TJ reached into her closet, pulled out the dress and tossed it on her bed. She didn't have time to go through the rest of her closet. She had to do her hair and makeup in less than… A glance at the clock and she gasped. Crap! Five minutes!

She dove for the bathroom and set to work on her hair, twisting and pinning it up in a quick French twist. After a dab of blush, a stroke of eyeliner and touch-up of mascara, she applied lipstick.

As she gave herself one last look at her reflection, the doorbell rang.

TJ raced into her bedroom and grabbed her dress. Then, hopping across the floor, she stepped into the garment as she hurried for the door. Before she reached for the knob, she inhaled a deep breath and let it out a little at a time, willing her heart to stop racing. Then she pressed her eye to the brass peephole.

Sean McNeal stood on the other side.

He took her breath away, ratcheting up her heart rate another five notches. From what TJ could see through the distorted image, she was going to be in for a heart-racing night.

Patting her hair in place with one hand, she reached for the doorknob with the other and pulled it open, school-ing her face into an expressionless mask. She hoped.

She wasn't prepared for the full impact of Sean McNeal in formal attire and fought to keep her jaw from going slack.

The black suit jacket was cut perfectly to fit Sean's broad shoulders and tapered in at the waist, emphasiz-ing the athlete. His thick black hair was smoothed back, one errant strand falling over his forehead like a sexy male model for a magazine.

Breathe, TJ, breathe!

Then he smiled. "You clean up pretty good." His gaze dropped to her feet. "Did you forget something or are you making a fashion statement?"

Blood rushed up her neck, heating her face as TJ glanced down at her bare feet. "I was getting to that detail when you rang the doorbell." She left the door open and walked away. "I'll be just a minute."

"Take your time."

His shoes made soft tapping noises as he stepped into the tiled entryway and the door clicked closed.

The last time he'd been in her apartment, he'd nailed a board over her broken window and then stayed the night holding her, but not touching her the way she would have liked. TJ dug in the bottom of her closet for her strappy silver sandals, blaming her rising temperature on the closeness of the small closet. Thoughts of what could have happened in the bed behind her didn't have anything to do with her inability to swallow or the way her body tingled all over.

No. Sean was a fling. Nothing more.

There. Deep in the back were the shiny sandals she searched for. She grabbed them and slipped them on. Now for a little jewelry. She didn't have an array of fine jewelry, but her mother had left her a single diamond pendant on a delicate platinum chain and matching diamond earrings. With an eye on the clock, she slipped the studs into her ears and then lifted the necklace around her neck.

"Here, let me." Warm, rough fingers relieved her of the chain and brushed against the base of her neck.

TJ stood with her breath caught in her throat, willing herself to stand straight and not give in to the over-whelming urge to lean back into Sean's arms. They had a job to do.

The necklace dropped into place, the diamond nestling at the top of her cleavage.

Sean's hands dropped to her shoulders covered only by the thin spaghetti straps of her black dress. The simple touch made TJ aware of just how little she wore.

Panties, dress, shoes and the rest was skin. Sizzling hot, begging to be kissed skin.

Was that a feathery brush of lips? Or was she imagining things, her mind playing on her wishful thinking? She swayed toward him.

"We'd better go." His words stirred the few tendrils that strayed from the French twist.

Disappointment settled in the pit of her stomach as she moved away from Sean. Was she crazy? She had a killer after her and all she could think about was the next kiss?

She dumped her driver's license, lipstick and money into a silver bag and finally found the courage to face Sean. "I'm ready."

He hurried her out the door to a waiting taxi, sure not to leave her exposed too long.

"Parking might be limited." Sean held the car door open while she stepped in and slid across the seat.

Great. He wouldn't have driving to keep him occupied, and she'd be fidgeting in the seat next to him. What if he asked her what was wrong? What would she tell him? *I'm the target of a maniac and I'm crazy about you. Isn't that enough?*

To avoid his questions, she launched the first one, keeping her voice to a level the taxi driver couldn't overhear. "What kinds of things are we looking for tonight?"

"We should keep our ears open for any reference to Frazier's death and any speculation about it, as well as any talk about the Millennium Challenge, Arobo or Dindi. When I get a chance, I'll duck into Crane's home office and see if I can find anything there."

"I'm going with you," she insisted.

Sean shook his head. "One person will draw less attention than two."

"Maybe so, but I want to know what's going on as well."

"You'd better serve as a lookout."

"But—"

He grasped her hands in his larger ones. "Please. Don't argue this point. I'd feel better if I were the only one caught in this game. Your job is on the line more than mine. I'm a temporary fixture in the Rayburn Building. You're not."

That shut her up for the moment. She couldn't argue with his reasoning. Even if she didn't like it, he was right. She'd already risked her job by sneaking into Crane's office and snooping through his files. "Okay, but I don't like you going it alone."

He smiled and lifted her hand to his lips. "I'll take that as a sign you care."

Though she liked the way his hand warmed her cold ones, she jerked free, afraid of getting used to having him kiss her knuckles and say nice things to her. "I do care. If you get caught, I might be implicated since we've spent so much time together in the past three days."

"Did anyone ever tell you, your forehead dimples when you frown?"

Before she realized what she was doing, her hand touched her forehead. She dropped it to push a strand of loose hair behind her ear. "Does not. You're just trying to fluster me and change the subject."

"Oh yes, it does."

When she opened her mouth to deny his words again, the car slowed for a turn.

Sean peered out the window. "Here we are."

TJ stared at the brightly lit home with the sweeping drive. The taxi curved around and stopped in front of the stone steps leading up into the mansion with the massive Roman columns and arched windows.

"Crane must like to flaunt his wealth." Sean slid out of the seat and bent to offer TJ his hand.

Accepting his assistance, she stepped out of the car and stood staring up at the double-door entrance. "Shall we?" Sean swept an arm in front of him and sketched a bow.

As TJ ascended the steps, her heart skipped a beat before it settled into a strong steady rhythm. With her senses primed to full alert, she entered the doorway on Sean's arm, ready to tackle this spy assignment thing. Bring it on!

TJ's LAUGHTER DRIFTED across the room to Sean. One congressman after another circulated past her, each wanting their chance to flirt with the beautiful woman they'd barely recognized as part of their everyday life. Classical music drifted through the room from the string quartet Crane hired for the event.

In that little black dress cut to mid-thigh, her legs seemed to stretch from her chin to her toes, no longer hidden by suit trousers, business skirts and sensible shoes. Her bare white shoulders had a slight dusting of pale freckles, sexy enough to turn any male head in the room. With her hair swept up off her neck, all Sean could think was how much he wanted to kiss her.

"How do you like working with Malone?" Gordon Harris stepped up beside Sean, a drink in his hand.

"She's smart and professional. What's not to like?" He shot a glance at Gordon before his gaze returned to TJ.

"She's a beauty, isn't she?" Gordon said.

Sean could have kicked himself for being so obvious and deflected Gordon's question with one of his own. "Congresswoman Malone?"

"No. TJ."

"Oh, yeah. I didn't notice." Lame. His response was completely lame. Where had his ability to maintain his cover gone? *South* with every other rational thought since TJ had opened the door in that short black dress.

Sean glanced her way and their gazes collided across the room. His pulse quickened and he wished they were back in her apartment instead of in a house full of strangers. He didn't relish making inane small talk while trying to discover which one, if any, of the congressmen there had anything to do with the Dindi bombing and Jason Frazier's death.

"You've been staring at her all evening, along with every other man in the room." Gordon shrugged. "Only difference is she stares back at you."

Gordon's gaze fixed on TJ. "I think what makes her unique is that she's completely unaware of her effect on men. She's a natural beauty inside and out."

"Yes, she is," Sean agreed.

"I'd sure hate to see her get hurt."

Sean's attention pivoted to Gordon and his brows rose in challenge. "Why would she get hurt?"

Gordon smiled and nodded pleasantly at one of Crane's assistants, before he continued, his voice low and intense. "Look, John, she's special. Don't break her heart."

Sean managed not to show his surprise at the statement. He snagged a wineglass from a tray as a waiter passed, then sipped from the glass. The wine was bitter, but he managed to swallow it without wincing. After a long pause, he turned to face Gordon. "You're in love with her, aren't you?"

"That's not the point." Gordon's lips tightened, the fingers around his glass turning white.

Sean almost felt sorry for the guy. He really was stuck on TJ. "And she's never been interested in you, has she?"

"I've known TJ for three years and in all that time, she hasn't gone out with any other man. No dates, no flirtations, just the job." Gordon's face flushed and his forced smile faded into a frown. "When you showed up, that all changed. I didn't put all the pieces together until I saw her staring at you tonight."

"Jealous?"

TJ laughed again at something a congressman said and both Sean and Gordon turned her way.

"Damn right." Gordon's gaze returned to Sean. "Tell me something. Were you the man she met in Dindi?"

"I don't know what you're talking about."

He moved closer. "Are you?"

Fighting the urge to step back, Sean answered in a smooth, controlled tone, "I've never been to Dindi."

"Don't bullshit me." Gordon's voice rose enough to get people to stare. He inhaled and let it out. "She was devastated by the explosion. She's been dragging around for the past month and not just because Haddock died. When you showed up, it was as if she'd come alive again. You're him, aren't you?"

Sean didn't have time to continue discussing TJ with

Gordon. He had a job to do. "I've only been in the
Rayburn Building for three days and I've never been to
Dindi. TJ's been nothing but polite and friendly, show-
ing me the ropes. That's all there is to it."

Gordon stared at him for a long moment, his eyes
narrowing. "I see." He set his glass on a nearby table,
spun on his heel and lost himself in a crowd of staffers.

Sean headed for the buffet filled with finger foods.

His mission at this party was to concentrate his investigation on Crane. Could it be possible a jealous
wannabe lover would contract a bombing in a foreign
country? Sean stopped and glanced back at Gordon. No.
It didn't make sense. If Gordon loved TJ, why would he
bomb an embassy she was supposed to be in at the time?

He reached for a small china plate and piled it with
gourmet crackers and little squares of cheese. Avoiding
the caviar, he opted for a miniature quiche, remembering he hadn't had dinner.

"Find out anything?" TJ's voice wrapped him in
tingling warmth.

"Not yet."

"What did Gordon have to say?"

"Not much." He didn't share his suspicions about
Gordon. Instead, he munched on a cracker before
asking, "What do you know about him?"

TJ smiled and that didn't settle Sean's misgivings
in the least.

"He's a good guy. He's been a legislative assistant
longer than I have and he helped me learn the ropes
when I started." She shrugged.

He swallowed the quiche in one bite. "Were you and
he ever a thing?"

TJ's lips curved upward and she tipped her head to the side. "I notice the two of you were pretty intense for a while there. What did he tell you?"

Sean ground his back teeth together. TJ had avoided the question. Why? Was she hiding a previous relationship with Gordon? Why couldn't she give him a straight answer? "Not much." *Just not to break your heart.* "Have you ever seen him get angry at anyone?"

Her eyes widened. "Gordon?" She chuckled. "He's as sweet as they come. And loyal to a fault. He can come on at times, but he's harmless. What's this all about?"

He polished off the crackers and laid his plate on an empty side table. "You should try the quiche." He dusted crumbs from his fingers and searched the room. "Where are Crane and Malone?"

"They're in the far corner by the senator from California."

"Good. I'm going in search of a bathroom." He captured her gaze. "Keep an eye on Crane."

When he turned to leave, her hand snagged his arm. "Wait."

"Yes?"

"I've never slept with Gordon, if that's what you're worried about."

"I'm not worried about anything." Although her confession did make him feel a little better, he didn't want her to get the wrong idea. He was an S.O.S. agent. He didn't have any business making long-term commitments to anyone. "Look, Barton, it's your life. You can sleep with anyone you want. Watch my back, will you?"

He left her standing there with her mouth open.

As soon as the statement had left his lips, he'd regretted it, but he'd squandered enough time staring at her and being sidetracked by Gordon. He had work to do before the party wound down. Already, people were expressing their farewells and heading for the front entrance. If he didn't hurry, he'd miss the opportunity to investigate Crane's office without being discovered.

Chapter Thirteen

You can sleep with anyone you want.

Of all the boneheaded things to say. TJ clenched her fists and struggled to keep her face from showing the anger pulsing beneath her skin.

As if she needed his permission to go to bed with anyone she wanted. Ha! She was a single adult, capable of deciding for herself.

"Ms. Barton, did you get a bad taste from something on the buffet?" Congresswoman Malone pressed her hand to TJ's arm.

"Ma'am?" TJ shook the man out of her head and concentrated on the congresswoman who'd garnered the respect of most of the women in the country, all the while sleeping her way to the top on the sly.

Because of Sean's last comment, TJ wanted to tell the member she could sleep with anyone she damned well pleased. But the cool, rational honest person inside TJ saw the injustice of what Congresswoman Malone was doing. A married woman had no business sleeping with Crane. The man was married to a kind and generous wife. As she stared at Mrs. Crane, TJ's anger simmered below the surface.

The motherly look the congresswoman gave her was enough to make TJ want to puke. "Really, you look like you swallowed a lemon."

"In a way I have." She forced a smile, certain it was more a grimace. "If you'll excuse me, I need a drink." She pushed away from the member before her mouth got carried away and she said what she really thought.

Where was Congressman Crane? He'd been on the far side of the room a few minutes ago, away from the hallway leading, hopefully, toward the study.

TJ didn't see any sign of Sean. He must have slipped out. But had Crane slipped out as well? And if so, where to?

Despite her previous ire and initial distrust, she didn't want him caught sneaking through the congressman's belongings. She made her way across the room as quickly as she could without appearing as if the house had caught fire.

By the time she reached the hallway, she hadn't seen Crane for so long, worry set in. Sean could be in real trouble. Armed with Sean's excuse of looking for the bathroom, she ducked her head in every room down the wide hallway. She found a parlor, a music conservatory, a billiard room and was beginning to think the study was on the second floor when she finally reached the last door on the hall.

Just as she turned the doorknob and poked her head inside, voices sounded at the other end of the hallway. TJ ducked through the doorway and peered through the tiny crack.

Congresswoman Malone stood with Crane, their heads close together, their words too low to hear. As they turned to walk toward TJ, Judith Crane stopped them and smiled graciously, laughing at something her husband said. She didn't have a clue what was happening beneath her nose.

"Looking for someone?" a deep, rumbling voice said next to TJ's ear.

TJ jumped and would have squealed if Sean's hand hadn't clamped over her mouth.

By the time her heart returned to her chest, he'd loosened his grip, his hand falling to her shoulder. "What's going on?"

"Crane and Malone are in the hall, possibly headed this way."

Sean pressed his face to the crack in the doorway. "They're not there now." He turned back toward the huge wooden desk in the center of a spacious office paneled in a deep red mahogany. Bookshelves reached floor to ceiling on two walls, lined with law books, biographies of past presidents and history books, all bound in rich leather.

"Have you found anything yet?" TJ stayed close to the door, keeping watch.

Sean pushed at the drawers on the desk.

"No. I can't get the one on this side to open. There doesn't appear to be a lock."

"The desk looks old. Many pieces of antique furniture had hidden locks. You have to look in other drawers or under the middle of the desk to find the release button. Here, you watch the door while I look."

TJ felt around the outer edges of the massive desk and then sat in the chair. Where would a master furniture maker put a switch that could be easily accessed but not seen? She opened the drawers she could and reached inside feeling around the underside of the desktop. A small, smoothly rounded wooden dowel dipped down from the desktop. TJ pushed it and the locked drawer sprung open half an inch.

"Good job, Barton. Only you better close it up. We've got visitors coming."

TJ sucked in a breath, her pulse racing. She carefully shut the drawer and set everything the way it was when she'd started.

Sean moved the sofa away from the corner far enough so they could both duck behind it. "Come on."

As voices sounded outside the study, TJ leaped for the corner and Sean pulled the sofa close to the wall to hide them. "We have to stop meeting this way," he whispered against TJ's hair.

Once again, her career was on the line and her nerves were a jittery mess. Despite it all, TJ's strongest desire at the moment was to giggle. She pressed her knuckles to her lips and fought to control the urge.

Sean's arms wrapped around her and pulled her close. "Are you okay?" His warm breath stirred the hair against her neck. With her skin and body sensitized to everything, the feathery touch tickled.

"It's okay, sweetheart." Sean's whispered words warmed her.

She wanted to shout, *No, it's not!* But she couldn't while trapped behind a sofa with two influential members of Congress on the other side. Two members involved in a love affair—and who knew what else.

"You have to support me in this." Crane's voice rose. "I won't have a member of my party vote against this proposal."

"Thomas," Congresswoman Malone said, her voice that of a mother talking to her teenager. "You have to let me handle this my way. I know what I'm doing. I won't vote yes until the final report is presented to the subcommittee tomorrow. Until that time, I'm letting everyone think I'm against the Arobo proposal."

"I need you to back this request, especially since Jason Frazier's death today."

"Such a tragedy." Malone sighed. "I wonder who would shoot him point-blank in the head?"

"Who knows?" Crane's tone was impatient. "Your denial undermines my authority and credibility on the committee. If you don't start letting everyone know you're for it, I'll…I'll…"

"You'll what?" Congresswoman Malone's voice took on the hard edge everyone in the Rayburn Building knew. When she used that tone, people scattered in all directions to avoid her wrath. The normally calm, collected woman was well known for her intolerance of idiots, a fact carefully kept hidden from her constituents, but not her staff.

TJ cringed, waiting for Crane to cut Malone down to size in a single sentence.

"I don't know what I'll do." Crane changed from the hard-nosed member of Congress to a pushover in a matter of seconds. "Just do it because you love me, will ya?"

TJ squirmed, hating the smarmy sound of Crane's tone. Why didn't he tell her which pier to jump off and kick her butt out of his house?

Where Malone had a low tolerance for idiots, TJ had an even lower tolerance for spineless fools who thought charm could win votes over intelligence. From the way

Crane bowed down to Malone, he was more a spineless fool than the strong-willed congressman TJ had assumed he was all these years.

But then what did she expect from a man who cheated on his wife while in office?

"Look, sweetheart, the party is almost over," Crane said. "I need to see my guests off."

"You go. I have a bit of a headache. If you don't mind, I'll stay here a while longer."

"Stay as long as you like. I'll let you know when most of the guests are gone."

Silence stretched and TJ thought, for a moment, they'd left.

A feminine moan sounded in front of the sofa. "Do you think Judith suspects anything?"

"Judith?" Crane laughed. "She's as clueless as my constituents."

TJ's stomach knotted. Poor Judith, the woman behind many successful children's hospital fund-raisers and book drives for the underprivileged. She even volunteered in soup kitchens in the less affluent areas of D.C. She had a heart of gold, but was married to a buffoon.

"Good. Neither one of us can afford a scandal." She paused. "We never know who might be our next president."

"President Crane." The congressman's voice sounded like an announcer at a public speech. "President Crane. It sounds right. Do you think I have a chance?"

"Anything's possible," Malone said. "Right now, you need to see your guests to the door so we'll have time to meet later." Her voice ended in a sultry purr.

"Oh, yes. I'll be back shortly. Don't go anywhere."

The door to the study creaked open. "Take something for that headache. There's some ibuprofen in the top middle drawer of my desk and a water decanter next to the Scotch."

"Thanks. Now, go on."

The door to the study clicked shut and the room fell silent.

"Go with him," TJ whispered a quiet entreaty. If Malone stayed in the room, TJ and Sean would be stuck lying on the floor behind this sofa for who knew how long.

Sean's arm tightened around her.

She could get used to being trapped in tight situations with Sean. The adrenaline high only added to her already overactive attraction to the man. If they weren't worried about making noise, and if Congresswoman Malone wasn't on the other side of the room…

The possibilities were titillating.

Wait, TJ. Weren't you supposed to be mad at Sean for his earlier comments about sleeping with anyone you wanted? She thought for a moment. No. The anger was gone and in its place was the overwhelming realization she only wanted to sleep with Sean. Now!

THE MORE SEAN WAS TRAPPED with TJ, the more he realized he liked being trapped with her. It was the only time he couldn't reason his way out of her presence. His rational mind had to accept she was going to be with him until they got out of the situation. In the meantime, his hand curved around her waist.

She leaned into him, resting her head in the crook of his shoulder. The scent of herbs and springtime drifted upward. No cloying perfumes for her, no layers of heavy makeup. In her simple black dress, she could crook her finger and he'd follow her anywhere.

He fought the urge to smooth a hand over her silk-clad hip.

"Think she's still in here?" TJ whispered.

He didn't care if Malone was or not, he didn't want to move from behind the sofa just yet. Outside this room, there were too many other commitments and distractions pulling TJ away from him.

Springs squeaked, like those of Crane's office chair.

That answered TJ's question. They couldn't leave until Congresswoman Malone left, which wouldn't be much longer. If Crane didn't come back until most of the guests left the party, they might have to wait even longer before they could sneak out undetected.

A hollow wooden pop, followed by the sliding sound of a drawer being pulled out made its way to Sean's ears. What was Malone up to? Was she searching through Crane's desk for the painkillers or for something else?

Electronic beeps were followed by Malone's voice as she spoke into her cell phone. "Hi, honey. After I leave Thomas's party, I'm headed back to my office. I've got a lot of work to catch up on. I should be home around midnight, no later... Don't wait up... I will." A click and the conversation ended. The chair springs squeaked again.

Sean held his breath. The study floor was carpeted. He couldn't hear where she was headed. If Malone happened to sit on the sofa and look over the back, Sean and TJ would be caught. Different scenarios sped through his mind. He could grab TJ and kiss her if

Malone saw them, saying they'd searched all over for a place to make out. But after all they'd overheard, Malone wouldn't buy it.

TJ tensed in his arms. If their cover was blown, word would get out that she couldn't be trusted. Where would she ever get another job in D.C.?

The S.O.S. Agency? She was former FBI, she knew how an organization like S.O.S. operated. Would she consider coming to work for Royce? The thought of working with TJ on a more permanent basis made his chest tighten. Maybe she'd finally forgive him for lying to her in Dindi.

His arm flexed, pulling her snugly against his body. The more he held her, the less he wanted to let her go. The chance of Malone finding them paled next to the thought of losing TJ.

The study door creaked open. "Hurry, the stragglers are leaving. You can sneak out with them." Crane's urgent tone sounded from the hallway.

"Are we meeting later?" Malone asked.

"You bet. Give me a few minutes to clear out the waitstaff and I'll be on my way."

"Good."

"I take it your headache is gone?" Crane's low laughter drifted across the room.

"Completely. It's as if I never had one."

The study door closed and Sean let out the breath he'd been holding.

"Whew. That could have been close." TJ pushed against the floor to sit up.

Sean's hand shot out and held her down. "Wait."

The hall door to the study creaked open again and

Malone's voice carried to them. "I'm pretty sure I left it by the desk."

With his hand still resting on her hip, Sean held his breath and strained to hear Malone's footsteps, cursing the carpeted floor for doing a good job at noise reduction. The light went out and finally the door to the study closed.

"Give it a few minutes to make sure no one else comes in," Sean whispered.

Her chest rose and fell with the deep breath she inhaled and let out. "This is all so cloak-and-dagger. How do you do it all the time?"

"It's the adrenaline fix."

She laughed. "I can understand. My adrenaline has been in hyper drive since we stepped into this office. You think it's safe to climb out from behind this sofa now?"

The house was quiet, the string quartet long since disappeared. Sean inched his way through the dark study, thankful for the subtle night-lights placed throughout. When he reached the door, he pressed his ear to the raised wood panels.

Nothing.

He eased the door open and cringed at the creaking that accompanied it.

Crane stood at the front entrance, shrugging into a dark coat. "I have a few things to deal with at the office. I'll be back around midnight."

Judith stood in front of him, adjusting the collar of his jacket. "The party was a success?"

"Yes, it was wonderful." He pressed a kiss to her forehead. "Thank you for all your work."

"It was my pleasure." Smoothing her hand down his

lapel, she sighed. "Don't be long. I don't like it when you work late."

"I know." He tapped a finger beneath her chin. "Is everyone gone?"

"Yes. I sent the waitstaff home a few minutes ago. They'll be back in the morning to clean." She kissed him once more. "Will you set the alarm when you leave?"

"I will." He buttoned one button and turned away from his wife. "Don't wait up."

Sean's heart skipped a beat. Alarm? Damn. He eased the door closed.

"What?"

"He's about to set an alarm." Sean scanned the room for an outside exit. Drapes covered one wall from floor to ceiling. He hurried across and pulled them back, revealing a set of double French doors. "We have to get out before he sets the alarm."

"But we haven't searched the drawer." TJ ran across the room and popped the lock for the secret drawer.

"We don't have time."

"But there might be something important in here." She flipped a penlight on and shuffled the pages aside until she made it to the bottom.

Sean hurried back to the study door and opened it enough to hear what was going on down the hallway.

An electronic voice echoed across the expanse. "Please enter your security code."

"Nothing," TJ said behind him. "No wait, I found something."

"We have to get out. *Now*." Before he could shut the study door, he heard another sound.

"Your perimeter alarm is now activated."

Chapter Fourteen

TJ leaped from Crane's desk chair and dove for the French doors.

Sean pivoted from his position by the hall door. "Don't touch that door."

TJ's hand jerked back from the knob and she stared across at Sean, her eyes wide, her heart stopped in her chest. "I thought we had to get out in a hurry."

"Too late."

"What do you mean, too late?"

"The perimeter alarms are set." Sean frowned. "If we try to get out of the building, the alarms will go off and every cop in the city will converge on this house."

"You're kidding, right?" She could tell from the set look on his face he wasn't.

"No. We're here until someone turns the system off."

TJ's heart sped up again, blood rushing from her veins so fast it made her dizzy. "How are we going to explain our way out of this?"

"We have one of two choices." Sean moved across the room and leaned against Crane's desk. "We can leave, set off the alarms and run like hell. And if we do, there's the chance of getting caught. Or we can stay and wait until someone turns off the security system, and then exit quietly through the French doors with no one the wiser." His lips twisted in a half smile. "I'll leave the choice up to you."

TJ's instinct was to choose the first option and run like hell. But after thinking through the scenarios, she realized a quiet exit would be the better choice. "Okay, we stay. I don't want the congressman to know someone is lurking around his home looking for something. It might alert him to the fact people are on to him."

Sean straightened and strolled around the room. "Crane told his wife he'd be back around midnight. If we play our cards right, we can get out when he comes in."

TJ stared at her watch. "That's a couple hours from now. What do you propose we do in the meantime?" Ideas popped into her head and her cheeks heated. TJ had to work on her poker face. Among Sean's other talents was mind reading and she couldn't afford for him to think she wanted to make love to him. A thrill of excitement skimmed across her senses. What was it about danger that made her want Sean even more?

Sean crossed the room and stood in front of her. He lifted her hands in his. "We don't have to do anything. So relax." Those big, rough hands squeezed hers. "Hey, what's this?" He held her hand up to the meager light.

His question penetrated her haze of lusty thoughts and she stared down at the card in her hand. "Oh, yeah. I found it in the secret drawer. It was standing up against the side, I almost missed it. I think you'll find it interesting."

Sean took the card and turned it over. "Damn."

"St. Croix Financial Services" was written in bold letters across the middle.

"Trey Masterson aka Eddy Smith," Sean said.

"How soon can we get that interview?" TJ asked.

"Could be tricky. Especially if the cops are on to him. However, Royce has connections with the D.C. Police. I don't think it'll hurt to check status on that front." He flipped his cell phone open and punched a single number.

TJ admired Sean's dark profile accentuated by the moonlight. The lighting made him appear even more dangerous than his usual dark, sultry look. James Bond had nothing on Sean McNeal.

"Royce, this is Sean. Is Tazer still on Eddy?" He paused to listen. "Good. She's great for the job... Yeah, we're okay... No, we can't come by the office right now." He stared across at TJ, a smile curving his lips. "We're in a tight situation, but we'll get out... No, we can handle it. Will do."

He flipped the phone shut and dropped it in the inside pocket of his suit jacket. "Royce says Eddy has a reputation with the ladies. Or at least he thinks he does. He's at an Irish pub in Adams Morgan." Sean grinned. "He put Tazer on him right after we found Jason. If he's a ladies' man, he won't know what hit him when Tazer sets her sights on him."

The curve of Sean's lips made TJ smile. "Tazer's the one who found out who rented the canoe, isn't she?"

"That's her. A deadly combination of beauty and intelligence."

A sting of jealousy pinched TJ's gut. "You'll have to introduce us."

"I will." Sean nodded. "I think you'd like her."

She'd probably like her better if she looked like an old sow. "Are you close to all the S.O.S. agents?"

"Mostly the ones I've worked with on assignments. But we look out for each other. We're small enough we all know everybody on a personal basis. It's like a family."

"Small is good. Sometimes, the bigger the organization, the smaller you feel inside."

"Like the FBI?"

"Yeah. After I lost my partner, I realized I didn't know many others in the Bureau. Not really."

"Why did you leave?" Sean's voice was low, steady, inviting her to open up.

For the first time in years, she wanted to let it out. "I didn't see the point. We weren't making a dent in the crime world and brave men and women died or were severely injured every day trying."

"What happened to your partner?"

A lump formed in her throat and she swallowed hard to force it down. Even after three years, she felt the pain as if it were yesterday. "I had the flu. I hadn't been sick the entire time I was at the Bureau until that day. My boss told me to stay home. They put a rookie agent with Mike." She snorted. "A rookie. Forensics finally got a match on the DNA samples from the victims of a serial homicide case we'd been working. They went after the guy, he shot Mike and the rookie. The rookie died, Mike was paralyzed and the killer got away. A senseless waste of good people." TJ turned away and crossed to Crane's desk. "I quit the FBI. End of story."

"Did you love Mike?"

TJ stiffened, keeping her back to Sean. Did she love Mike? "I thought I did. No, I know I loved him." She turned and faced him. "I loved him like you loved Marty. He was my partner and as close as a friend can be. He depended on me and I let him down."

"You can't blame yourself. You weren't there."

Her brows rose. "And do you blame yourself for Marty's death? You weren't there."

Sean's lips formed a thin line. "The two situations were different."

"I had the flu. I probably could have made it in that day."

Sean shoved a hand through his hair. "I wasn't sick, I was...distracted."

"You couldn't be there all the time. What if the embassy had blown while you were out to lunch or gone to the bathroom? You can't be there all the time. It took me years to figure that out."

"I'm beginning to. I just need more than a month to let it go."

TJ nodded. "I know." She stretched, rolling her shoulders and neck. "Can we put the past behind us? I find it exhausting."

"Consider it in the past."

"Good." She made a pass through the room, inspecting book titles as best she could in the near dark. When she'd run out of patience for squinting, she looked across at Sean. "So now all we can do is sit tight and wait until midnight." Her gaze landed on the sofa in the corner. "We could sit on the sofa and duck behind it if someone walks in." And it was big enough for two. Cozy. Not that she had anything other than sitting in mind. Especially since she was in a congressman's house for less than honest reasons.

Sean sat on the sofa and patted the seat beside him. "Come on, I won't bite."

"Darn, I was hoping you would." Now that the danger was on hold until midnight and they were alone in the room, butterflies filled TJ's belly. All the time she'd been afraid of being caught in Crane's house wasn't nearly as frightening as sitting next to Sean on the couch.

She hesitated. "On second thought, maybe I'll stand guard by the door, in case someone decides to come in for a little light reading. You never can be too careful when you're breaking and entering." Okay, now she was babbling. She clapped a hand over her mouth to keep other inane comments from escaping.

"What are you afraid of, TJ?"

"Other than being caught in a place I don't belong and possibly going to jail? I can't see that I should be afraid of anything." And really, she wasn't. For the first time in years, she felt energized by her actions. More energized than working as a legislative assistant ever made her feel.

No, she was more afraid of a black-haired, green-eyed bad boy with room enough for her beside him on the couch.

He patted the seat next to him. "Then come sit with me and we can go over what we've learned so far."

Oh, so this wasn't a seduction attempt? Her disappointment killed the butterflies. She trudged over to the couch and sank onto the leather cushions, tugging at the short hem of her dress. With her nearly bare thigh only inches from Sean's, her mouth dried and she fidgeted with her bracelet. When Sean reached out and patted her hands, she jumped.

"As much as I admire that dress and you in it, I'm not going to jump you. So relax."

She frowned and pulled her hands away from his. "I'm not afraid you'll jump me. Whatever gave you that idea?" She felt like her heart was a yo-yo, bouncing up into her throat and down into her belly with each word Sean spoke.

"Never mind." He released her hands, resting one arm across the back of the couch and the other on the armrest.

TJ laid her hands in her lap and fought to keep them still. "So, what do we have?"

"One bombing in Dindi. Money wired to the terrorist from a bank in the Caribbean Islands." Sean stared at the ceiling, his brows pressed together. "The account that wired the money to Dindi is owned by St. Croix Financial Services."

TJ picked up the laundry list. "Two payments from T.O. Enterprises to the St. Croix Financial Services account under Trey Masterson around the time of the bombing. Jason Frazier was one of the investors in T.O. Enterprises. I saw Eddy in Dindi prior to the explosion. We think we saw Jason and Eddy together in a canoe before they shot at us."

"Then Jason was shot in the head some time over the past twenty-four hours. The potential for oil off the coast of Dindi and Arobo could be the driving factor."

"Now this." TJ held up the St. Croix Financial Services card, loosely linking T.O. Enterprises and Congressman Crane, who had a lot to be gained with the Dindi bombing. He now had the opportunity to push Arobo's Millennium Challenge funding.

"We've learned a lot in the past few days." TJ leaned back, the stress finally catching up to her. What she wouldn't give to be home in her own bed.

"Still, it's not enough—we don't know if it goes even higher than Jason and Eddy."

"What do you mean, we don't know?" TJ held up the business card. "What do you call this and the documents in Crane's office?"

Sean leaned forward, resting his elbows on his knees and pressing his fingers together in a steeple. "Do you get the feeling this might be all too obvious?"

"No." TJ yawned and shook her head. "I think Crane is in it up to his eyeballs and we should nail him to the wall for killing Haddock and your friend Marty."

"And if we're wrong and we blow the whistle on the wrong set of suspects, our real ringleader gets away."

TJ closed her eyes for a moment. "This is all confusing. We need to have a conversation with Eddy Smith. I suspect someone contracted him directly to do the bombing. If we could force a confession out of him, we could sew up this case. Maybe he would accept a plea bargain and confess to who paid him."

"And maybe pigs will learn to fly."

TJ smiled, her eyes still closed. Now that they were in wait mode, fatigue had taken hold, slowing her ability to think and making her eyelids very heavy. A yawn welled up in her chest and escaped. "I'm sorry. I can't seem to stay awake."

"Rest your eyes. I'll wake you when Crane comes in."

"But we weren't finished talking about the case."

"We've done enough. We know we need to find Eddy and have a little conversation with him."

"Yeah. Talk to Eddy." She yawned again. "Okay, I'm going to rest my eyes for a few minutes. But only for a few. You sure you're not sleepy?" She forced one eye open but didn't bother to lift her head off the cushions. "I could stay awake if you want me to keep watch." Although how she'd do that, she didn't know. After last night's maybe two hours of sleep, the lack of rest had finally caught up with her.

Sean smoothed the hair back from her temples.

"Ummm. That's nice." She liked the way his fingers felt. Gentle, yet firm.

"Rest," Sean murmured. "I'll take care of you."

His low voice soothed her even more and she leaned against his shoulder. "Don't need anyone to take care of me." She kicked off her sandals and curled her feet on the seat next to her.

"No, you can handle everything on your own."

"You—" she yawned "—bet."

SEAN TIPPED TJ OVER until her head lay in his lap.

She breathed in the deep steady rhythm of one sound asleep. Her face relaxed, her lips curling into a smile. One slim hand crept up between her cheek and his leg.

With her warm body beside him, Sean was filled with a longing so strong, he had to move.

Sliding her head from his leg, he stood and tucked a soft pillow beneath her cheek.

Then he paced back and forth across the carpet until the threads lay flat.

The clue they hadn't discussed scared him more than any of the others. Someone had attacked TJ outside her apartment. Had it been Eddy Smith? And if so, TJ had no business chasing the guy down for answers. He might turn the tables and make her his next victim.

Sean stared down at the sexy woman in the tiny black

dress, sleeping like a child. How could he let her put herself in harm's way?

She'd once been an FBI agent, trained in self-defense and interrogation techniques. She *could* handle herself, as she'd proven when the man attacked her in her apartment last night. Just that afternoon, he'd considered her a good candidate as an S.O.S. agent and daydreamed about working side by side. But with killers like Eddy Smith running loose, he wasn't so sure anymore.

No, he had to get TJ out of this mess. Once the case was solved, he'd face the decision of what to do about his growing attraction for the sandy blonde with the deep brown eyes.

The sound of a door opening down the hall jerked Sean out of his dreams about the future and back to the congressman's study. A glance at his watch revealed it was only eleven. Could Crane already be back from his meeting with Malone? Sean ran to the hall door and eased it open.

Congressman Crane stepped through the door, juggling his briefcase. When he pulled the keys from the lock, he dropped them on the tile.

If they wanted to escape, they had the next few seconds to do it.

Sean hurried to the couch and shook TJ. "Crane's back."

She sat up, her eyes wide but cloudy. "What?"

"If we want out, we only have about five seconds before he reactivates the alarm. Let's go." He scooped her shoes from the floor and grabbed her hand.

As he reached for the knob to the French doors, he took a deep breath and twisted it. He stood for a moment, listening. No alarms. Good. With a quick jerk, he opened the door and shoved TJ through. Sean stepped outside and turned to ease the door closed.

"I'll take those." TJ grabbed the sandals from Sean's hands and slipped them on to her bare feet. "I wish I'd brought my tennis shoes. Looks like we'll be climbing through a few hedges to get to the street. You can go first to blaze the trail."

Pushing through a tall hedge, Sean held branches aside as TJ picked her way through in the impractical heels. When they finally stood on the street, he snagged her hand and walked as fast as she could go, putting as much distance as he could between them and the Crane house.

Once they were several blocks away, Sean flipped open his cell phone and called a taxi. TJ couldn't go much farther on those heels. Although she hadn't said one word of complaint, she favored her right foot.

"Where to?" TJ asked, bending to remove one sandal. She stood with one foot flat on the sidewalk. "Ahhh. Much better."

That she was game to keep going only made Sean more determined to give her a break. "You're going home to bed." He stared across the cell phone at her, giving her a narrow-eyed look.

Her brows rose on a smooth forehead.

"Alone," Sean amended.

Brown eyes narrowed into slits and she crossed her arms over her chest. "And you?"

Damn, she was pretty when she was stubborn. Pretty and irresistible. "I'm going after Eddy."

She slipped her shoe back on her foot. "I'm going with you."

"No, you're not. You look like you're dead on your feet."

"You really know how to compliment a girl." She rubbed her hands over her bare arms. "I'm going."

He crossed his arms over his chest and glared at her. "Over my dead body."

She held up her hand when he would have said more. "That's what I'm hoping to avoid."

Chapter Fifteen

TJ sat in silence on the taxi ride into Adams Morgan. After she'd threatened to come on her own, Sean had given in. Not happily, by a long shot, but he'd agreed to take her with him.

He'd called Tazer's cell phone and she'd told them she'd found Eddy at O'Reily's Irish Pub. The noise in the background was too loud for much more information than that.

As the taxi pulled in front of the pub, Sean leaned over the seat and handed the man a twenty. Then he slid out and rounded the vehicle to open the door for TJ.

Still in their cocktail-party garb, they looked like any other overdressed couple coming for a late drink. Sean's hand rested on TJ's elbow and they were just about to go inside when Sean's cell rang. He dug the phone out of his pocket. "Hey, Tazer."

TJ leaned into Sean's shoulder to listen in on the conversation, but street noise and the rumble of music from inside drowned out whatever Tazer said.

"Sounds good." He flipped the phone closed and stuck it in his breast pocket.

"What's the plan?" TJ asked.

"Tazer's got Eddy's interest. We should be able to get in without him noticing us. Ten minutes after we get inside and have a look around, she'll offer to leave with him. We'll meet her out in the alley."

Her heart leaped. Finally, she'd have answers.

"Don't get your hopes up. He's likely to resist our efforts to interview him."

"I'm sure, between the three of us, we can manage."

"I want you to stay clear and let me and Tazer handle him."

TJ gave him an exasperated look. "What does Tazer have that I don't?"

"A mean right hook." Sean grasped her shoulders and leaned close. "If I'm worrying about you—"

"You'll be distracted and blow the deal." TJ's mouth firmed into a thin line. "You'll have to learn to work with distractions." She held her hand up. "Don't worry, I'll let you and Tazer handle Eddy."

A group of young people spilled out of the bar, laughing and calling out to each other.

Sean pulled TJ into his arms and kissed her.

When he let her go, she stood still for a moment to regain her balance.

Sean hooked a hand beneath her elbow and led her up the stairs and into the bar without another argument. Once inside, the spilled alcohol and blare of Irish folk music cleared her brain.

As Sean steered her through the crowd, he leaned close and whispered in her ear, "Eddy's by the bar."

TJ looked across the sea of faces to a bulky, dark-haired man with an oversized nose, the one she'd seen in front of the American embassy and on the towpath.

At that exact moment, Eddy glanced their way.

TJ pulled Sean behind a wooden pillar. When two couples rose from a booth in a dark corner, TJ and Sean slid into the empty seats.

Their waitress, a young woman dressed in black pants and a drink-stained white blouse, stopped at the table to collect the empty mugs and wineglasses. "What'll ya have?"

"Guinness," Sean answered.

"I'll have the same." Anything to get rid of the waitress blocking her view of Eddy.

When the young woman walked off, Sean leaned across the table. "There's Tazer."

A woman wearing low-cut, tight jeans and a cherry-red tube top swayed through the crowd. Her long, straight blond hair was pulled back in a loose ponytail tied with a black silk scarf. She captured every man's attention as she worked her way to the stool beside Eddy. Leaning close, she twirled her fingers across his neck and whispered in the big guy's ear.

TJ's jaw slackened. "That's Tazer?"

"That's her."

Wow, if ever a woman was well put together, S.O.S. agent Tazer was perfect in every way. With the cool, pale-blond sex appeal of Sharon Stone and the body of a goddess, she was lethal. Eddy didn't stand a chance.

The hired killer practically drooled, along with every other guy in the place. But Eddy was at least twice Tazer's weight. What would she do if he attacked her?

"Will she be all right?" TJ asked. "I mean, he was one big, strong guy when he attacked me at my apartment."

Sean smiled across the table and shook his head. "Yes, he is a big guy. I'm still amazed you were able to get away from him."

Her brows dipped. "I told you—"

"You've been trained in self-defense." He raised his hands as if to deflect her next volley.

"I've been trained, but how much does Tazer know about self-defense with guys the size of Eddy?"

"Trust me when I tell you, she can handle him, no problem." He leaned close. "I've seen her take down a three-hundred-fifty-pound football jock in under ten seconds. Had him crying like a baby."

TJ's lips twitched and despite herself couldn't hold back the smile. "Jocks are a piece of cake. Can she handle a hired killer?"

"She can handle anyone." He looked toward Tazer, all humor gone from his face. "When it comes to picking a bodyguard, I want her on my team."

As long as that was all she was—a bodyguard. Tazer had the equipment to be a whole lot more.

The waitress returned and plunked two pint glasses full of creamy stout on the table in front of them. "You want me to start a tab?" she asked.

"No need." Sean paid her and she disappeared.

TJ leaned forward. "When do we make our move?"

Sean took a long pull of his beer and swallowed. "We want this to look as natural as possible." He reached across the table and took her hand in his. "We're supposed to be a couple out on a date."

TJ laughed. "Some date."

One at a time, Sean pressed his lips to her fingertips. "What? Don't you like the atmosphere?"

She shrugged and looked around. The noise was almost deafening with everyone laughing and trying to talk above the music. "I'd rather be in a quiet little bistro with soft background music."

"Like that place we found in Dindi?" He still held her hand, only now he threaded his fingers through hers, locking them in an intimate clasp. "The one two blocks over from your hotel?"

"Yeah." She lifted her gaze to his and the rest of the room disappeared. Instead of a busy pub filled with the raucous calls of college students and the too-loud men watching baseball in the corner, she was back in that café.

The more she stared into his deep green eyes, the more she realized how much of an impact he'd had on her even then—before he "died." She wouldn't have forgotten him in a couple days or even months.

He lifted her fingers to his lips again and pressed a kiss into her palm. "Just make me one promise."

Promise? He wanted a promise from her? She swallowed, but nothing could get past the lump in her throat. "And what's that?"

"Don't make any decisions about us until we solve this case." His fingers tightened around hers. "Deal?"

"Deal."

Well, what did she expect? It wasn't as if Sean McNeal, S.O.S. agent, would want her to promise to love, honor and cherish him until death do us part. She broke eye contact and stared across the room. "Uh, Sean? When did you say Tazer was going to make her move?"

Sean's head jerked around and he was on his feet at the same time as TJ rose to hers. "Damn." He was already striding toward the door, passing his cell phone to her. "Speed dial two and tell Royce Eddy's on the move."

He barreled his way through the crowd like a linebacker, shouldering his way to the door. A young man shouted something rude. Sean wasn't listening.

TJ shot the guy a dirty look. "Get over it." While moving toward the door, she flipped open the phone and punched the number two. Then she was outside, standing in the cool night air.

Sean ducked down the alley next to the pub.

TJ pressed the phone to her ear and ran after Sean. Ducking into the dark alley, she saw two people standing in the shadows. Sean and Tazer. Laying at Tazer's feet was Eddy Smith.

"Is he dead?" TJ asked.

Tazer shook her head. "No, only unconscious." She sounded disappointed. "He shouldn't have tried to grab my top. I like this top." She stared down at the red fabric and brushed off an imaginary speck of dust.

Sean smiled at Tazer. "Didn't even break a sweat, did you?"

She shrugged and stared at a fingernail. "Some things are too easy."

"Sean?" Royce Fontaine's voice sounded in TJ's ear.

"No, this is TJ. Sean asked me to call and tell you Eddy's on the move. Only he's not now. He's down."

"Is he dead?"

"No, Tazer assures me he's still alive."

Royce breathed a sigh. "Good. I'll send a car over to pick him up."

After TJ gave him the address, Royce said, *"Good job, team."*

When the head of the S.O.S. agency hung up, his words echoed in TJ's ears. Good job, team. He hadn't meant her, but she felt like she'd been part of the team even if she didn't bring Eddy down. How long since it had felt this good to be a part of a team?

Tazer pulled a tight roll of two-inch silver duct tape from her purse and tore off an eight-inch strip.

TJ grinned. "You always carry duct tape?"

The gorgeous blonde shrugged. "Never know when it'll come in handy."

"When you're done with Eddy, mind showing me what you did to knock him out?" A healthy dose of envy struck TJ.

Kneeling beside the unconscious body, Tazer slapped the tape over his mouth. "Any time," she said, then un-buckled her belt.

Sean knelt beside her and rolled Eddy over to his stomach, jerking his arms behind his back.

Tazer looped her belt around Eddy's wrists and cinched it tight. Then she removed the long silk scarf from her neck and tied it around the man's eyes. She straightened, brushing her hands together.

"I have a feeling I could learn a lot from you," TJ muttered.

"Nothing any woman couldn't do, if she has a mind."

As a long black limousine eased to a stop at the end of the alley, Eddy stirred.

The driver, an ultra-sexy Latino with soft brown eyes and rich dark hair, sauntered over to Tazer. "I hear you caught a big one, *mi amor*." He captured her hand and kissed her knuckles.

Sean winced. "Valdez, you're treading on thin ice, buddy."

"Ah, but our Tazer is *muy bonita*." When he bent to kiss her knuckles again, Tazer jerked her hand free.

"Save your shtick for girls who buy it." Tazer walked over to Eddy. He tried to lift his head, but she pressed her shoe to his face, nailing his cheek to the pavement. "Down, boy."

The smooth-talking man converged on TJ. "Ah, the beautiful TJ. Where have you been hiding?"

"Ignore him, TJ. He has a genetic defect that he can't take no for an answer." Sean shoved between Valdez and TJ, breaking the man's hold on her. "Let's get him loaded before he starts making noise."

The men each grabbed one of Eddy's shoulders and hauled him into the backseat of the limousine.

Tazer stood beside TJ. "Casanova Valdez fancies himself a heartthrob. The only thing he makes throb on me is my head."

TJ struggled to keep a straight face. "He's got the right name and the looks for it." Although flattered by his flowery words, Valdez wasn't her type. Her tastes ran in a different direction. Her gaze shifted to Sean.

Once Eddy was loaded, Tazer stood with Sean and TJ. "I'll take shotgun."

That left Sean and TJ to ride in back with Eddy.

The short ride sped by in silence. Eddy lay on his side on the long backseat, struggling to get his hands free.

When they arrived at the S.O.S. office complex, the

limo pulled into the parking garage and into a com-pletely enclosed space with a private elevator.

Valdez and Sean hauled Eddy out of the backseat. This time, Eddy put up a fight.

"If you give us too much trouble, we'll shoot you," Sean said. "No one will care. In fact, I'm sure the law will consider it a public service."

Valdez laughed. "Maybe they'll give us an award or something."

Their threat didn't slow Eddy down. His feet kicked out and landed sharp blows to Sean's and Valdez's shins. Their grunts accompanied them into the elevator. When TJ would have followed, Tazer grabbed her arm. "Let's take the next one."

The shiny chrome doors shut, TJ and Tazer standing in the garage.

Tazer stood for a moment staring at the closed elevator doors. "So, what is it with you and McNeal?"

TJ wished she could answer the woman's question for her own peace of mind. "Me and McNeal? We work together at the Rayburn Building, that's all."

"But you're the woman Sean met in Dindi, right?"

TJ rolled her eyes. "What's with you guys? Does everyone know everything about each other in this or-ganization?"

Tazer turned to her, her beautiful face set in tight lines. "Kat Sikes is my friend. The night before Marty died, he called Kat and told her about how happy he was Sean had met a woman he could be serious about."

TJ bit back an automatic denial. Hadn't she thought the same? When she'd met him in Dindi and thought he was a businessman, they seemed perfect for each other.

Given his real occupation, chances were high he'd end up like Marty.

Being with Sean these last couple days had served as a reminder of what she was missing from her days as an FBI agent. Granted, she'd put up with a lot of politics and bullshit. But the knowledge that she was doing something for the good of others, the interesting challenges and an occasional chase had kept her going.

However, she liked helping congressmen make policy. It was mentally challenging, and…and mentally challenging. *Face it, girl. You're bored out of your mind.*

She turned to Tazer. "Do you ever get tired of this job?"

One of Tazer's finely arched brows rose. "I'm sorry, is this a job?" Her lips curved into a secret smile. "I thought it was going out for a little fun."

"No really. Do you see yourself ever doing anything different?"

"Look, TJ, I like what I do. When I get tired of doing it, I'll do something else."

"And how long have you been doing it?"

"Five years."

"What about relationships, marriage, family?"

"When that time comes, whoever I marry will have to be willing to accept me no matter what I do." Her voice dropped into a mutter. "As if that will ever happen."

TJ heard the words, though she guessed she wasn't supposed to. She suspected that despite the woman's amazing looks she'd had her share of disappointments. "Did your parents name you Tazer or is it a nickname?"

"What does it matter? I like the name. It makes guys think twice before they mess with me."

The more she talked with the female agent, the more TJ wondered what she hid behind her tough exterior. The elevator bell rang and the brushed chrome doors slid open.

Tazer shot another glance at her. "Sean's a nice guy. Don't hurt him."

"Is that a threat?"

"Call it a suggestion."

They accomplished the elevator ride in silence each staring straight ahead.

When the doors slid open, Tazer stepped out. "The observation room is this way." She strode through the maze of offices and cubicles to a door at the far end of the floor.

Valdez stood inside, staring through a large window overlooking a sparsely furnished, brightly lit interrogation room. Sean and Royce stood to one side of the room. Eddy was center stage, seated in a hard plastic chair, still bound by Tazer's belt and blindfolded by her pretty silk scarf. Someone had removed the duct tape allowing Eddy the opportunity to speak. And Eddy Smith had a mouth. He used every curse word TJ knew and a few she didn't.

Royce and Sean waited for Eddy to run out of steam. When he finally did, Royce spoke first. "Eddy, who hired you to bomb the embassy in Dindi?"

"I don't know nothin' about no bombing, you stupid moth—"

"Look, Eddy. We already have enough evidence to put you in prison for the rest of your life, so you might as well cooperate. You might get a lighter sentence if you tell us who paid you to do it."

"I ain't tellin' you nothin'. I wanna see my lawyer."

"We don't deal in lawyers here. We take care of business," Sean said. "We like to call it a one-stop-shop. Judge, jury and executioner all in one. Care to change your answer?"

"I didn't bomb nothin'."

"Then where did the five hundred thousand dollars come from in your business's bank account?" Sean leaned close to Eddy's ear. "That's a lot of money for a guy from the wrong side of the tracks."

"Not enough." He snorted.

Royce stepped up to Eddy. "Did Jason Frazier pay you to do the job?"

"He's dead."

"Who do you think they'll pin with his murder?"

"Much as I couldn't stand that lying, cheating bastard, I didn't kill Frazier. Someone got to him before I could, or maybe I would have."

Sean and Royce exchanged a look over the top of Eddy's head.

"The same person who paid you to hire Manu for the Dindi bombing?" Sean asked.

"I don't know what you're talking about." Eddy clamped his lips shut and didn't speak another word.

Sean leaned on the arms of the chair and spoke in Eddy's face. "You think this person you're protecting would return the favor? I'll bet you the five hundred thousand dollars that whoever paid you to bomb Dindi would turn you in faster than you could yell foul."

No matter how much Sean and Royce talked, Eddy refused to cooperate. He sat with his lips tightly sealed.

After another forty-five minutes of frustration, Sean and Royce left Eddy by himself and stepped into the observation room with Tazer, Valdez and TJ. They were arguing and brought the argument with them.

"I say we turn him over to the police and let them do the investigation," Sean said. "We have enough evidence to put him away for good."

"True," Royce responded. "But you and I both know he's covering for someone, and it isn't the late Jason Frazier."

"Why don't you turn him loose?" TJ stepped forward.

Sean looked at her like she'd sprouted horns. "He's a killer. He killed Marty and Congressman Haddock."

She nodded and rested a hand on Sean's arm. "Turn him loose and he'll either warn his backer or demand more money to keep quiet."

"She's got a point." Tazer stepped up beside TJ. "If we want to catch the real culprit, Eddy might just be the one to lead us to him."

"We'll put someone on Eddy 24-7," Royce said. "We'll know his every move."

As the S.O.S. agents talked to and around her, TJ felt included in their little group, and she liked it. She liked being part of their team. Working at the Rayburn Building with all the stuffy, egotistical politicians was becoming less and less appealing.

SEAN WASN'T HAPPY with the idea of letting a known killer loose. "I don't like it. The guy's a criminal. He's responsible for blowing up the embassy, for killing Marty and almost killing TJ. I can't believe you want to let him go."

Royce touched a hand to Sean's arm. "We have to find out who's at the bottom of this. As clearly guilty as

Eddy is, someone else besides Jason Frazier called the shots. Jason was involved and met justice. You want the other guy to walk away?"

For a long moment, Sean digested Royce's words. On the one hand, they had to find the backer. Whoever started this deal ended up killing Congressman Haddock and Marty. Sean owed it to Marty and Kat to find him and put him in jail.

Then he glanced across at TJ. Her face was flushed, her eyes bright. He'd never seen her quite so animated, as if she relished the challenge.

Was everyone in the room crazy except him? "Who are you putting on Eddy?"

"Valdez and Tazer." Royce nodded to the pair. "Take him back to his car and turn him loose. But stay on him. And, Tazer?"

"Yes, boss?" the blond beauty answered.

"Change before you go. You're like a red flag to a bull."

Tazer gave Royce her slow sultry smile. "Like the outfit?"

Royce nodded. "Yeah, it's memorable. And take the listening equipment. My guess is Eddy will look for a way to contact his backer."

Tazer turned to leave the observation room. "I'll be back in a minute. I'm just going to slip into something less comfortable."

Although he knew the idea had merit, Sean couldn't stand the thought of Eddy running loose in the city. "I'd like to follow him as well, at least until I'm due back at the Rayburn Building."

"Then I'm going with you," TJ insisted.

"You're going back to your apartment to sleep." The

night ahead would be long and boring, following a man who'd probably go home to bed.

"You're my protection, remember?" Her brows rose and she gave him a slow, smug smile. "I go where you go."

Royce chuckled. "You two follow for a while, but don't be too obvious. He's bound to figure out we're watching him and get real slippery."

"Does Tim still have some of those GPS tracking devices?"

"Someone talking about me?" Tim Trainer called out from the hallway.

Sean shook his head. "Do you have radar imbedded in you?"

"It's a gift." Tim joined them. "Got new GPS devices in yesterday. I'll have them to you in two shakes." Tim jogged down the corridor and returned in less than two minutes. He handed Sean a disk the size of a dime and another device that looked like a cell phone.

Tazer returned wearing a black leather jacket zipped up over her red tube top, her hair tucked beneath a baseball cap.

Tim handed her another of the cell phone-like gadgets. "You stick the chip on your target's body some-where he won't find it easily and you can follow him anywhere with the GPS locator."

"Ready?" Sean stared around at Tazer, Valdez and finally TJ.

"I'm ready," TJ said. "Let's get this show on the road."

Sean stuck the GPS locator in his pocket and headed for the interrogation room and the burly hit man he was going to turn loose on D.C. He hoped the hell he was doing the right thing.

Chapter Sixteen

TJ glanced at the digital clock on the dash and sighed. One minute had passed and it seemed more like ten.

Then Valdez ran from the alley and around the corner to where Tazer waited. Sean emerged from the alley right behind him and jogged toward the car. He jerked the door open and slid in. "Kill the engine and duck." Sean slid low in his seat and peered through the window.

TJ turned the ignition key and leaned over the console.

Sean ducked lower. "Here he comes." He pulled the GPS tracking device from his pocket and switched it on. A map of the streets appeared with a light blinking in the middle. The light was moving slowly, then it took off. "He must be in his car." Sean sat up. "You want me to drive?"

"I know the streets. I can handle it." TJ turned the key and the car roared to life. "You're the navigator, lead the way."

"He's headed toward Columbia Road, and he's moving fast."

TJ slammed her foot on the accelerator and the car

leapt out into the street, arriving at the first intersection in time for a red light.

With no one in front of her, TJ ran it and sped on.

In the seat next to her, Sean clutched the console. "You sure you don't want me to drive?"

"Positive. Where to next?" She gripped the wheel, loving the surge of power beneath her feet, her adrenalin racing with the car's engine.

"Left on Columbia, heading south."

At Columbia, TJ was forced to cool her engine behind four other cars waiting for the light. She chewed on her lip, shooting glances at the GPS locator. "How far is he?"

"He just hit Dupont Circle and now Hampshire."

The light changed and traffic crawled forward. TJ zigzagged through the vehicles and shot southward on Columbia, cutting off on Florida then 32nd, hoping to catch Eddy at Washington Circle.

"He just turned off Hampton onto M Street."

But there they were, stuck at another light.

As they waited for the traffic to move, Sean gave her the blow-by-blow. "He's headed down M Street, now Canal."

The light changed and TJ eased forward behind six other vehicles. "Why are all these people still awake? Don't they know it's past time to go home to bed?"

Sean chuckled in the seat next to her. "A little road rage building there?"

"A little is putting it mildly. Where is he now?"

"Passing Georgetown."

"I bet he takes Key Bridge out to the beltway."

"Nope, he just passed Key Bridge and turned back onto Whitehurst Freeway."

"What?" TJ shot a glance at Sean. "You think he knows he's being followed?"

"I don't know, but this doesn't make sense. He's stopping."

"On the freeway?"

"No, wait, he must be on K Street, below the freeway, and he's moving very slowly now." Sean flipped his cell phone open and punched a number. "Valdez, where are you two? Okay… It looks like he might be moving on foot in the vicinity of K Street and 33rd… No, we can handle it, just let me know when you get close."

"Where are they?" TJ's blood carried adrenaline to every cell of her body.

"Someone caused a three-car pileup on Dupont Circle. They're stuck in the traffic. Our guy is headed toward the river."

TJ pulled onto K Street, slowed and then turned south on 33rd.

Sean put a hand out to touch her arm. "Slow down. He stopped."

TJ parked the car against the curb and cut the engine.

"I'll go on foot from here." Sean pulled a Glock from the glove box and chambered a round before he stepped from the car.

TJ got out, too. "No, I'm going with you."

He frowned and then turned and ran down the street toward the river.

TJ followed. Even with danger just around the corner, TJ couldn't help smiling. She liked getting under Sean's skin. Especially since he was so firmly beneath hers.

Tires squealed and a loud thump echoed off the buildings lining the waterfront. Then a shiny black car sped by on the street below.

Had the thump been that of Eddy climbing into a car and shutting the door? Had he gotten away? TJ slowed, hesitating between running back for the car and moving toward the river.

Sean continued his headlong race down the hill toward the river.

Even though she'd changed into running shoes and jeans, TJ couldn't keep pace with him.

He turned right on the river road and disappeared out of sight.

Her heart in her throat, TJ pushed harder until her lungs burned. When she cleared the visual barrier of the buildings, she searched the street for Sean. For a moment, she didn't see anyone. Then she saw a man bent over next to the side of the road half a block away.

Sean?

TJ stumbled and for a moment she couldn't think or breathe. Was Sean hurt?

On level ground now, she stretched her legs and ran as fast as she could. The light from the streetlamps didn't reach this far and TJ couldn't make out who was there.

"Sean!" All thought for her own safety took a back-seat to her worry for Sean.

The man straightened and TJ could tell he wore a black suit and he was tall and athletic, not bulky and stout like Eddy. This man was Sean and he held open his arms.

TJ collapsed against him and buried her face in his shoulder. She breathed in and out, catching her breath and inhaling Sean's aftershave. The scent comforted her at the same time as it disturbed her. When her breathing was under control she pushed back enough to look up into his eyes. "For a moment, I didn't see you."

"I'm fine." He cradled her in his embrace, smiling down at her.

"Of course you are." She didn't step away, or let go of him. She'd died another thousand deaths in the few seconds she'd lost him, the same desperation she'd felt when the bomb exploded in Dindi, choking off her air. "I kinda like having you around."

"Same here." He smoothed the hair that had tumbled into her face. Then he claimed her lips in a tender kiss. When he broke off, he cupped her face in his hands. "What am I going to do with you?"

"I don't know, but you'll have a hard time getting rid of me now." She wrapped her arms around his waist and held on tight.

"Tazer and Valdez will be here soon and we have to figure out what happened to Eddy."

"Where is he?"

Sean tipped his head. "Right behind you."

TJ's heart bounced against her ribs and she spun in Sean's arms, braced for attack.

But Eddy Smith wasn't attacking anyone. His motionless body lay against the curb.

"Is he dead?" TJ asked.

"Yeah."

"How?"

"That car that came by a moment ago plowed right into him."

"An accident?"

"No, the headlights were shining dead on." Sean's arms tightened around TJ. "Whoever hit him meant to kill him."

SEAN WALKED TJ INTO her apartment, wondering how he could leave her and head back to his own place in the S.O.S. building. When she looked up into his eyes, she had him. He couldn't leave her. Not after Eddy's death and the round of questions from the cops. With morning only a couple hours away, he didn't want to leave.

"You don't have to stay if you don't want to." TJ's voice was breathy. "But after what happened tonight, I have to admit, I'm a little scared."

He pulled her into his arms and held her. When holding wasn't enough, he lowered his head to claim her lips, as if by kissing her he could erase all the death and deceit happening around them.

Her fingers curled around his neck and she returned his kiss, her tongue tangling with his.

The next thing he knew they were stumbling across the living room, items of clothing hitting the floor with every step. Shoes went first, then TJ's shirt and Sean's jacket.

"Are we insane?" TJ unbuttoned Sean's shirt, slid it from his shoulders and tossed it in the corner.

"No doubt." He stood before her in his dress slacks and nothing else. "If you want to back out, now's the time to do it." He prayed she didn't. As tight as his zipper pressed against him, he wouldn't make it back to his car. A slow walk around the block wouldn't cure the ache inside.

Wearing nothing but her lacy black strapless bra and panties, TJ slid her fingers around the metal clasp of his trousers. "I'm not backing out, and don't think you'll get away that easy." She tugged the clasp loose, applying enough pressure to unbalance him.

He moved forward until his thighs touched hers, the

hard ridge behind his zipper pressing against her hands. "Nothing short of a bomb would make me leave now."

TJ's hand shook as she trailed the zipper downward. "Don't even think it." She pushed his trousers and his boxers over his hips and they dropped to the floor, his rigid member now pressing against the soft skin of her belly.

TJ sucked in a breath, a smile curling her lips.

Sean reached behind her and fumbled with the hooks on her bra.

"Don't they teach you anything in agent school?" TJ shook her head. "Here, let me." With a quick flick of her fingers, TJ had the clasp undone and the bra dropped to the floor, her breasts spilling free into Sean's palms.

He circled her nipples with his thumbs, loving the way they puckered into tight peaks. His fingers slipped beneath the elastic of her panties and he eased them over the swell of her hips and well-toned thighs. He dropped to one knee and worked the silky garment past her ankles, lifting one foot at a time to release the silken scrap, while pressing a kiss to the inside of each knee.

Now that TJ was completely naked, Sean set out to reacquaint himself with all those places he'd explored in the hotel room in Dindi. Starting with the sensitive area along her calves, his hands moved upward, smoothing a path for his lips to follow.

TJ moaned, reaching out to lace her fingers through his hair. "Seems we've been here before."

"I remember this scar." He pressed a kiss to the knee with the thin white line of scar tissue.

"Bicycle accident, age ten." She sucked in a breath as his tongue flicked over the sensitive skin of her inner thigh.

Sean liked it when her body tensed at his touch. With

the sweet scent of her desire, his pulse quickened, sending a rush of blood south. He stood, scooped an arm beneath her legs and swept her off her feet.

TJ draped an arm around his neck and giggled. "Are they teaching *How to be a Neanderthal* in agent school?"

"No, it comes with the Y chromosome." His lips dropped to her nearest breast and he sucked the nipple between his teeth, biting down gently.

"Ummmm. Thank goodness." She crooked a thumb over her shoulder. "The bedroom's in there. Can we get there before morning?"

"Ready for this to be over so soon?"

"No, I'm ready to get started." She planted her hands on each side of his face and kissed him, drawing his tongue out to play.

When he came up for breath, Sean realized he couldn't wait any longer. He had to have her. Now.

He strode the short distance across her living room to the bedroom and laid her across the bed, lying beside her on the comforter. "Now, where were we?"

Her hand slipped down his torso and she grasped him between her fingers. "I think we were getting to this point."

Though his entire body rejoiced at her touch, he wanted to prolong the moment and bring her as much pleasure as she brought him. "What? No foreplay?"

"It's overrated." She tugged him toward her. "I want you, Sean McNeal, John Newman, whoever you are. I want you inside me, now."

"Bossy ex-fed." He alternated nipping at a nipple then laving it with his tongue, loving the taste of her skin. "What if I'm not ready?" he breathed over her damp peaks.

She answered with an indelicate snort. "Yeah right.

Come here." Then with surprising strength, she dragged him on top of her. "That's better."

Their lovemaking was fierce and passionate, as if all the danger and death around them fed their lust and made them hungry for life and the living. Much later, when they'd collapsed in the bed, spent and satiated, he held her close.

TJ laid with one arm across his chest, a leg draped over his thigh. The gentle flow of her breathing feathered across the hairs on his chest. As exhausted as Sean was, he should be sleeping, but sleep evaded him.

Their only link to who'd contracted the bombing was dead. Although Sean wasn't sad to see Eddy die, he was concerned they now were back to square one.

What clues had they missed? Where should he start looking? Crane's concealment of the oil engineering report made him seem like a likely suspect. Perhaps they should put a bug on him and track his movements. But what else?

His arm tightened around TJ, her silky soft skin warm against his. He couldn't let anything happen to her. She'd become too much a part of his life again.

Think! The only clues they really had were those associated with the bank transfers and the engineering report from Arobo. There had to be something they'd overlooked. T.O. Enterprises had more investor names on that list than Jason Frazier.

Sean slid his arm from beneath TJ and slipped out of bed. He had to see the list of investors again. Maybe there was a name they'd overlooked.

After dragging on his slacks, white shirt and shoes, he scratched a quick note on a napkin and laid it on the pillow beside TJ. Slinging his jacket over his shoulder, he left her apartment, locking the door behind him. TJ would be up within the next fifteen minutes. She'd been certain Eddy had been the one to attack her on both occasions. With Eddy out of the picture, she should be all right. Once he was outside her apartment, he called Royce for a backup to follow TJ to work.

As the gray light of dawn crept over the Capitol, a taxi dropped Sean in front of the S.O.S. building. He'd called ahead to wake Tim. They had work to do if they were going to solve this case before the evidence grew cold along with the bodies.

He found Tim in the computer lab. Before Sean could say good morning, Tim jumped in. "I've been going over the list, one name at a time, since yesterday. So far, everyone checks out. No skeletons in the closet or criminal records." He clicked on an icon and a corporate Web page displayed. "However, one of the investors is actually another corporation. I'm still hacking to find out who belongs in it."

"Let me know what you find. Do you have hard copies of the cell phone pictures I gave you from in Crane's office?"

"Sure." Tim rifled through a file and unearthed several documents, handing them to Sean.

"I keep thinking we might have missed something." He glanced down at his watch and swore. "Congresswoman Malone will expect me at work on time. She'll just have to wait."

"Is the congresswoman that hard to work with?"

"No, not really." He wasn't so much worried about the congresswoman as he was TJ. Eddy knew TJ could identify him as the man leaving the embassy. She'd been a threat to him. Were there others afraid of her questioning? "Hey, also go back through Eddy's phone records—home, business and cell phone. There has to be a call we're missing."

Tim nodded. "I'll get right on it."

"And I need another GPS tracking device for a vehicle. I wasn't able to get the other one off Eddy's before they towed it to the impound lot. I want to record all of Congressman Crane's movements, just in case he's our guy."

"I'll see about retrieving Eddy's, later. In the meantime…" Tim opened a desk drawer and pulled out a box full of gadgets. He handed him a small rectangular metal box. "This one has a powerful magnet. You stick it somewhere on the car and track it with this." He handed him a device similar to the one he'd used to track Eddy.

"Thanks, Tim." Sean jammed the devices into his pockets and headed to his apartment for a shower and clean clothes. The suit he'd worn the night before smelled of cocktail party and a dead man.

Chapter Seventeen

When the alarm blasted through her sleep, TJ hit the snooze button and rolled back to the center of the bed, feeling for Sean. The place where he'd slept was empty. TJ's eyes cracked open and she noted the indentation and rumpled sheets. No, it hadn't been a dream, although the sex was something dreams were made of. She smiled and reached out to hug the pillow Sean had slept on. That's when she found the note.

"Gone for a shower and change of clothes. See you at work. S."

"Well, what did you expect?" she grumbled out loud, tossing the sheets aside to walk straight into the bathroom. After a shower, she brushed her hair and climbed into her work clothes. Her normal routine struck her as odd. With two people dead and having been attacked on more than one occasion in the last two days, work seemed low on her priority list.

Brushing aside thoughts of Sean and ideas of how to solve the case, TJ kept a watchful eye on everything around. It added up to an uneventful drive to the Rayburn Building.

TJ entered her office, dumped her purse in a drawer and strode back out, bumping into Gordon Harris in the hallway.

"TJ." He grabbed her upper arms to steady her. "Where are you going in such a hurry?"

"I had some questions for Congressman Crane." All evidence pointed to him.

"He's in his office getting ready for the Appropriations Committee meeting tomorrow. They're going to put the Arobo MC funding to a vote."

"Good. That's what I wanted to talk to him about."

"He's not in the best mood. I just got my head chewed off for not having a report to him."

TJ grimaced. "How long have you known about it?"

Gordon glanced at his watch. "Exactly ten minutes."

"Ouch." Crane didn't scare her, but how receptive would he be to her questions? He'd threatened her last time she'd tried to get information out of him. Would he fire her on the spot for being so forward this time? Not that she'd miss her job, but she'd lose access to the Rayburn Building if she were canned. "Thanks for the heads-up, Gordon."

Despite the congressman's foul mood, TJ strode in the direction of Crane's office, determined to get to the bottom of the Dindi bombing and Jason and Eddy's deaths.

Staffers scurried around like nervous rats inside Crane's suite. Everyone had their heads down as if the lower their profiles, the less likely the congressman would yell at them.

TJ swallowed, hoping the burbling in her belly would stay down until she'd had her conversation with Crane.

She met no resistance at his receptionist's desk. It

was empty. Crane's office door was closed but his voice boomed from within.

After a quick glance around to ensure she was alone, TJ turned the knob and pushed the door open enough to see inside, but hopefully not enough to draw attention to herself.

Crane had his back to her, pacing the floor in front of his desk, his face glowing a splotchy red. "I'll kill her, I tell you. I knew this would happen. I told her she needed to demonstrate her support of the funding or others would cave as well. What good does it do to have the party leadership in a committee if your party doesn't stand by your decisions? It undermines my authority. I won't have it!"

Guilt didn't enter TJ's thought processes. If Crane was responsible for the bombing, TJ would do anything to nail him, including eavesdropping.

Crane's voice lowered. "That's where you come into it. I want her off the committee. Do whatever it takes. Do you understand? Whatever. It. Takes. Just get her off."

As Crane turned toward the door, the bottom dropped out of TJ's belly. As quietly as she'd opened the door, she pulled it closed. When she let go of the handle, the catch clicked. Damn.

"What the hell?" Congressman Crane's voice could be heard moving toward the door.

TJ searched the outer room for a place to hide and ducked into the knee-space of Crane's secretary's desk as the door jerked open.

Footsteps stomped by the desk. "Look, I have to go. I might have a little situation on my hands," he said.

TJ held her breath, her knees to her chin, hoping Crane didn't see her crouched beneath the desk.

After several long moments of silence, TJ ventured a glance around the wooden desk panels.

No sign of Crane.

She scrambled from beneath the desk and out into one of the busy outer offices where legislative assistants shuffled papers and barely looked up when she passed through.

Out in the hallway, TJ hurried away from Crane's suite. Whew! That was close.

What did Crane mean by do whatever it takes to get her off the committee?

The "her" he referred to had to be Congresswoman Malone. She'd said she would publicly oppose the Arobo Millennium Challenge up until the last day. Would Crane have her killed because of her open opposition? Wasn't that taking it a bit far?

But then what had happened to Jason Frazier and Eddy Smith? If Crane had used them to orchestrate the bombing to clear the path for the Arobo deal and then killed them to maintain their silence, why wouldn't he kill another person standing in his way?

No. A congressman didn't kill people. These people didn't get their hands dirty themselves.

Whatever. It. Takes.

TJ shook her head. All their spying and snooping could have given her the wrong interpretation of the situation.

But what if Congressman Crane *had* just signed the execution order for Congresswoman Malone? Didn't TJ have the responsibility to pass that information on, even if it wasn't correct? Malone had a right to know she might be the next target of a crazed killer.

She had to find Sean.

Between the two of them, they could explain their concerns to Congresswoman Malone and she'd understand. From there, Malone could decide whether or not the threat was real.

TJ stopped in front of Sean's desk. Neat stacks of paper rested in his in-box. It was empty.

She ducked into the rest of the offices searching for Sean. When she reached Malone's receptionist's desk, she stopped. "Have you seen John Newman?"

"No, he hasn't come in yet. Do you want to leave a message?"

"No." She stared past the receptionist at Malone's closed door, chewing her bottom lip. Did she wait for Sean or should she go ahead and tell Malone what she knew? "Is Congresswoman Malone in?"

"No, ma'am. She said she'd be in around noon. The party last night wore her out."

Party my fanny. She'd been up late with Congressman Crane, and he was about to put the ultimate move on her if TJ didn't get to her first.

In TJ's race to the elevator, she passed Gordon in the hall.

"Hey, where are you going?" Gordon snatched at her arm and pulled her to a halt. "Slow down or you'll have everyone thinking the building's on fire."

Irritation flared. "Let go of my arm, please. I have to go. I need to get to Congresswoman Malone."

"Why?"

"When John Newman comes in, tell him I went to Malone's house and to follow me there."

"Her house? You know she discourages unexpected callers."

"She'll make an exception." TJ pulled loose of Gordon's arms. "Will you tell John?"

"Sure." Gordon frowned. "But I'd like to know what's going on."

"Another time. I'll tell you another time." TJ caught the elevator door as it closed, rushed in and punched the parking garage sublevel.

She had to get to Malone before Crane's henchman. The woman didn't deserve to die over funding for a foreign country. Even if there was enough oil to eliminate the United States' dependency on the Middle East.

Not until she'd pulled her car keys from her pocket and climbed into her car, did she realize she'd left her cell phone and purse in her desk. Oh, well, she had OnStar. If she needed a telephone badly enough, she could go through them. She didn't have time to go back to her office. If Crane wanted something done to get rid of Malone, he'd attack while she wasn't in the Rayburn Building. What better time than now? The sooner the congresswoman knew of the danger, the better.

Although TJ had lost much of her respect for the woman, she didn't wish her dead. The thought had crossed TJ's mind that Ann Malone might know of the oil engineering report in Crane's office. Had she been involved in the bombing?

No. Ann Malone was a tough contender in the political arena and she was having an affair, but that didn't make her a murderer.

Had Congressman Crane only been stringing her along in order to buy her vote? If so, the man was slime. Unworthy of political office and incapable of playing fair. But did that make him a murderer? Could she afford to take the chance that he wasn't? No. Crane might have another Eddy Smith on the payroll ready to perform his dirty work.

Having been to one of Ann Malone's informal gatherings, TJ knew where the congresswoman lived. Her Foxhall home wasn't far from Crane's.

Daytime traffic being what it was in D.C., TJ's driving experience was stop and go all the way, catching every red light and sitting through some for several light changes.

She could have chewed the leather off her steering wheel by the time she cleared the Capitol and shot out on Pennsylvania Avenue headed west.

TJ sped through the streets, conscious of her lack of a driver's license and cell phone. But then again, if a police officer tried to pull her over, she'd just keep driving and lead him to Malone's house as additional protection.

When she finally pulled up to the gate at Congresswoman Malone's home, she breathed a short sigh of relief and rang the bell.

A courtly sounding butler with an English accent answered. "May I help you?"

"This is legislative assistant TJ Barton. I need to see Congresswoman Malone. It's an emergency."

"One moment please."

TJ tapped her finger on the car's window frame, waiting impatiently for the butler to get back to her.

After several long minutes, the butler's voice said, "Please proceed to the front entrance, madam."

The black iron gate creaked open. As soon as it was wide enough to fit her car, TJ gunned the engine and shot forward, squealing to a halt at the front steps.

Once out of her car, she took the steps two at a time. Before she could raise her hand to bang on the door, it swung open and a tall, stiff man in a black suit bowed. "Congresswoman Malone will see you in the parlor. It's the first door on the left."

TJ hurried ahead of the butler to the door opening on an elegantly furnished parlor. Antiques appropriate to the period the house was built adorned the room, a tribute to the bygone era and the designer's exquisite taste.

When TJ stepped in, Congresswoman Malone rose from a Queen Ann sofa, her silky, navy-blue pantsuit perfectly tailored to fit. "Ms. Barton." She held out her hand and shook TJ's.

TJ glanced over her shoulder to the man behind her. "Could I speak to you alone?"

Malone nodded to the butler. "Please run that errand I asked, Galin."

"Yes, madam." He bowed and pulled shut the parlor door behind him.

Finally alone with the congresswoman, TJ didn't know where to begin. What had seemed so urgent in Crane's office sounded crazy now. One member of the House sending a hit man after another member? All over a little government funding issue?

"You said you had an emergency?" Malone settled back on the sofa and rested her hand on a throw pillow, twirling her fingers through the corded tassels.

"Well, yes." TJ gulped. If Malone was in trouble, really in trouble, she'd better spit it out. Should Crane's call turn out to be nothing, TJ would look stupid. On the other hand, if Crane was behind the bombing, he wasn't above killing a congressman to get what he wanted. Why not a congresswoman? Even the one he was sleeping with. "This might sound crazy, but I think someone could be out to kill you."

Congresswoman Malone's eyebrows inched up her forehead and a smile curved her lips. "Oh, really? And who would want to kill me?"

TJ's stomach burbled a protest for having skipped breakfast. Ann Malone had given her the reaction TJ should have expected. The congresswoman probably had threats on a daily basis just being in the Rayburn Building and working on Capitol Hill.

"I overheard Congressman Crane…" TJ stopped and thought through just what she'd heard. He hadn't mentioned a name, just a gender. What did she really know?

"Overheard what?" She smiled and waved at the wingback chair beside the sofa. "Come on, you've come all this way because you believe I'm in danger. I appreciate that. Have a seat and tell me what you know."

Her warm smile didn't fit with the war stories TJ had heard from Malone's assistants, but TJ needed the encouragement when self-doubt set in. "For the past few days, we've been trying to determine who was behind the bombing in Dindi."

"We?" Malone's eyelids narrowed.

TJ could have kicked herself. "I mean, I've been searching for the truth behind Congressman Haddock's death."

Malone's brows dipped into a frown and her lips pressed together. "Go on."

TJ carefully worded her next comments to avoid divulging her sources. "Information I received indicated the terrorist who set the bomb was paid by a hired killer from here in D.C., Eddy Smith."

"Interesting. Is that all?"

"I found out he'd been paid by a corporation called T.O. Enterprises of which Jason Frazier was an investor and a lobbyist. Jason and Eddy were murdered recently. I think Congressman Crane is behind all of it because he wants the Millennium Challenge funding for Arobo." There. She'd said what she came to say.

"Why is Arobo so important?"

Relieved Malone hadn't laughed her out of her house, TJ leaned forward, resting her hands on her knees. "There's oil off the shore of Arobo and Dindi. Engineers for Troy Oil have discovered an oil reserve that could rival that of the Middle East. I think Crane wants a part of that." Purely conjecture, she realized, but Malone had to understand what she was up against.

Her eyes narrowed into thin slits. "So that's what he's been hiding."

"The point is that I think Crane's willing to do anything to make sure Arobo gets that funding, including getting rid of the opposition, like Haddock." TJ stared at Ann Malone. "And you."

"So the bastard wants to get rid of me does he?" Congresswoman Malone stood and paced across the floor.

"You believe me?" TJ was a little surprised at how quickly the woman accepted what she'd told her.

"Of course. Crane's ruthless. He won't stop until he gets exactly what he wants. I voted against the funding for Arobo, but if he has his way, it'll go through." Congresswoman Malone halted her pacing and turned to face TJ. "We have to stop him."

"Should we take it to the police?"

"Yes, of course." Malone frowned. "Only I just sent Galin on an errand in my car."

"Why don't we call and have a detective meet us here?"

Malone waved a hand, dismissing TJ's suggestion. "Reporters tune into police scanners. They'd be all over us before the detectives left the office. No, we need to go to the police with this."

"My car's outside. We could take it."

"Excellent. Let me get my purse."

TJ followed the congresswoman into the hallway.

"Wait here. I'll be right back."

TJ stood in the empty foyer while Ann Malone climbed the staircase to the second story and disappeared down a hall.

When she returned, she carried a large handbag and she was slipping her arms into an oversized, hooded black coat. The hood totally hid the woman's face. "Can't have the press following us into the police station, can we?" She slipped a pair of sunglasses onto the bridge of her nose and smiled. "Ready?"

TJ settled behind the wheel and Ann Malone climbed into the passenger seat. When they pulled out of the drive, the congresswoman flipped her cell phone open and punched a single digit.

"Calling the office to tell them you won't be in?" TJ asked.

"Something like that." She listened for a few minutes and shook her head. "Damned answering machines," she muttered. "Thomas, something's come up. If you value your career, meet me at the cabin immediately."

TJ's foot lifted from the accelerator. "Thomas? As

in Thomas Crane? Did you just call Congressman Crane?" Suddenly the hooded jacket and sunglasses seemed sinister.

Malone turned sideways in her seat and smiled like it was the most natural thing in the world to call the man who wanted to kill her and tell him to meet her. "Yes, dear, I did. And we won't be going to the police station. We're going on a little road trip."

"I don't understand. We need to get to the police. Crane's trying to kill you." She slowed to a stop at a red light.

Malone's smile disappeared and the lines in her face appeared even more severe than after a trying day at the office. She tipped her hand up enough TJ could see the .38 caliber pistol resting in her palm. "Maybe you'll understand this."

Chapter Eighteen

Sean didn't see TJ when he arrived an hour late for work. He'd thought maybe she'd overslept and gave her another hour. Now he was passed worried, nearing panic. From TJ's empty office, he dialed her cell number. He heard it ring in her desk. Digging through the drawers, he found her phone and purse, but no keys.

She'd left in a hurry. Something must have happened.

When Gordon Harris stepped through the door, Sean practically pounced on him. "Have you seen TJ?"

"Well, yeah. She left shortly after she came in this morning."

"When did she come in?"

"Her regular time, I suppose."

Sean grabbed Gordon's arms. "Did she say where she was going?"

"Whoa, buddy, what's your hurry?" Gordon brushed Sean's hands free, frowning.

"If you care at all for TJ, you'll tell me where she is." Sean's hands bunched into tight fists. His gut told him TJ was in deep trouble and he had to get to her. Now.

"First, you tell me what the hell's going on here. She

ran out of here around nine-thirty this morning, as if the building was on fire." Gordon frowned at Sean. "Ever since you showed up, she's been acting strange. What's going on? What have you done to her?"

"I don't have time to explain and I haven't done anything to TJ." Sean drew in a deep breath and let it out slowly, striving for patience. "Did she say anything as she left?"

"Yeah, and that was what was so weird. As she ran off, she asked me to tell you she was headed for Congresswoman Malone's house and you were to meet her there."

"Why the hell didn't you tell me sooner?"

"I've been in a meeting for the past hour, or I would have. What's the big deal anyway?"

Sean had already pivoted, ready to run to the garage, when he thought again and faced Gordon. "Is Congressman Crane around?"

"He left about an hour after TJ. He told me to cancel all his meetings, he didn't know when he'd get back."

Sean didn't wait for more. Knowing Crane had suddenly left the building didn't make him feel any better about TJ's disappearance. He skipped the elevator and took the stairs two at a time to the garage.

Meet her at Malone's house? Not until he was in his car did he remember he needed her address. He flipped his cell phone open and dialed the S.O.S. office. "Tim, get me Congresswoman Malone's address, ASAP."

Within a matter of seconds, Tim had the address and phone number.

While negotiating the early lunch-hour traffic, Sean dialed Malone's home phone number.

A man with a British accent answered. "Malone residence."

"This is staff assistant John Newman, is Congresswoman Malone there? It's an emergency."

"I'm sorry, sir, she's not here."

"Do you know where she went? It's really important that I find her." *And TJ.*

"She didn't leave a note. I took Congresswoman Malone's car, so I assume she's with Ms. Barton."

If TJ had gone to Malone's and her car wasn't there and neither woman made it back to the office, where were they? Had Crane and Malone worked together on the deal to bomb the Dindi embassy and to kill Frazier and Smith? Or had Crane found out TJ and Malone were meeting and decided to invite himself?

Sean scrambled for the GPS tracker in his pocket. He'd stuck the magnet on Crane's car earlier intending for Tim to record Crane's movements.

The device, the size of a PDA, warmed up and a map displayed with a red blinking dot. Crane's vehicle was already outside the metro area and headed southwest toward Manassas.

Then he remembered TJ's car had OnStar. He dialed the S.O.S. office again. "Tim?"

"What's up, Sean?"

"Get a hold of OnStar and have them track TJ Barton. Tell them it's an emergency."

"Will do."

Sean started to put his phone down when Tim's voice came over the line.

"Oh, McNeal?"

He fumbled to seat the flip phone against his ear. "Yeah."

"I dug into one of the corporation names on that list of investors and found more interesting facts."

"What?"

"One of the corporations is owned by a Michael Malone from New York. Congresswoman Ann Malone's husband."

"Are you certain? Did you check to see that this particular Michael Malone is the one married to the congresswoman?"

"Yup."

The hard knot in Sean's gut became a lead wrecking ball, slamming around his insides. "Thanks, Tim. Will you connect me to Royce?"

Once Royce was on the line, Sean filled him in.

"You think Malone is behind all this?"

"That's what it looks like and possibly Crane." Sean pulled out into traffic and turned his car toward the freeway.

"Tim's here in my office. He says OnStar's located TJ's car. It's out in Fauquier County and it's stopped." He gave Sean the directions.

"I stuck a tracking device on Crane's vehicle this morning. Looks like he's headed that way."

"I'll send a team to back you up. Want me to call the police?"

"Not yet. I'm afraid they'll get there before us and do something stupid." The thought of TJ in the middle of a standoff turned Sean's stomach. "I'm thirty minutes behind Crane."

"We'll be fifteen minutes behind you. Don't do anything until we get there, if you can help it."

Sean shot out onto the beltway and pressed his foot to the floor. If he didn't get caught in a traffic jam, he might close the distance between himself and Crane. But he couldn't begin to guess what Malone might already have done to TJ. And he didn't want to. TJ had to be all right. She'd always told him she could take care of herself. Sean hoped she was right.

"CONGRESSWOMAN MALONE, Ann, you have to stop this now." TJ shifted the car into Park in front of a two-story cedar and rock cabin nestled deep in the woods of Crane's country estate. TJ assumed the congresswoman had met the congressman here on more than one occasion.

"I intend to stop it here and you're going to help me." She unbuckled her seat belt, snatched the keys from the ignition and slid from the car, sure to keep the gun leveled on TJ.

If she was going to break free, she had to do it before Crane got there. She braced herself to throw the car door open and run for it.

"Don't try anything stupid." Malone jabbed the .38 at her. "I know how to use this gun. Raise your hands where I can see them." She eased around the car, the gun aimed at TJ's head through the windshield. Once she'd made it around, she stood clear of the door, the weapon still pointed at TJ. "Get out."

With one hand raised, TJ lowered the other and opened her car door. She stepped out and quickly assessed the layout. Wooden steps led up to a wide, wraparound porch.

Malone waved the gun toward the house. "Inside. And hurry it up."

TJ mounted the steps and tried the door handle. It was locked. "Guess we'll have to wait for Crane."

"Move aside."

TJ stepped to the right.

Malone pulled a key from the pocket of her silk trousers and inserted it in the keyhole, all the while keeping the gun on TJ. When the lock clicked open, TJ lunged at Malone.

A shot rang out, hitting TJ in the shoulder. The force spun her and she slammed against the rough cedar of the porch column. Gray haze clouded TJ's vision, her knees caved and she sank to the wood deck.

She fought the darkness, knowing if she passed out, she didn't stand a chance of fighting back or escaping, not to mention she risked the possibility of bleeding to death.

"That was stupid, Ms. Barton." Ann Malone stood over her, with the gun pointed at TJ's heart. "I don't care if you're dying, get inside now."

Her vision cleared and she glared up at Malone. "You'll pay for that."

"I sincerely doubt that. I don't plan on paying for anything." She jerked her head to the side. "Now get in before I have to drag you in unconscious." Her hair and clothing still perfectly in place, the only things out of kilter on Congresswoman Malone was the intense gleam in her eyes and the feral tone in her voice.

TJ obeyed. She had to pack something against the wound on her shoulder, or she'd bleed out before she could fight her way free. Once on her feet, she swayed, afraid she'd fall again. Blood oozed down the front of her suit jacket, but despite the pain, she could move her arm.

With Malone behind her every step of the way, TJ entered through the open door and walked into a spacious living area decorated in warm browns, green and burgundy. She sank onto a bomber-jacket brown sofa and shrugged out of her jacket, wincing as she eased it over her wounded shoulder. When she saw the amount of blood on both sides of the jacket, her vision blurred again. Without looking at the other woman, TJ said, "I need something to stop the bleeding."

"No, you really don't. It'll only prolong the inevitable." The woman's voice was cool and emotionless, as if she was stating an uninteresting fact from an Appropriations Committee report.

TJ didn't consider her life an uninteresting fact. "What do you mean by that?"

"I mean I have to thank you for falling into my plan beautifully."

TJ had already gathered Malone was involved in the bombing incident in Dindi, what she hadn't figured out was why. "What plan?"

"Why should you care what my plan is? You'll be dead soon."

Sucking in a breath, TJ willed her heart to slow. Her death would come sooner if she didn't tame her hammering pulse. She needed time to think. "If you're going to kill me anyway, what would it hurt to tell me?"

Malone's gaze narrowed, and for a moment TJ thought she'd refuse. Then the woman shrugged. "You're right. What will it hurt? I plan to be the chairwoman of the Appropriations Committee."

"What?" TJ shook her head. Congresswoman Ann Malone had definitely gone over the edge. "How is killing me going to make you head of the Appropriations Committee?"

"Because I'm not going to kill you, Congressman Thomas Crane is."

"Why would he do that?" TJ pressed her jacket to the wound on her shoulder, determined to stop the flow of blood and hang on to consciousness. This story was getting more bizarre by the second and she wanted to be around to hear the congresswoman out.

"Don't be an idiot. You were smart enough to figure out the connection between the Millennium Challenge and the Dindi bombing. I'm sure others will put two and two together once I leak the information to the press. They'll assume Thomas hired the terrorist to bomb the Dindi embassy. Not only because of the oil reserves off the coast of Arobo, but because he was next in line to be chairman." Malone gave a soft laugh. "It was rather brilliant of me to have Eddy bomb the Dindi embassy with Haddock inside, don't you think?"

"You were responsible all along?" Why hadn't she thought of Malone? "What about Jason Frazier's death? Was that you, too?"

"Pretty smart wasn't it? I got Jason to hire Eddy to do the job in Dindi and then I took care of Jason with Crane's gun." She waved the pistol in her hand, a smug smile on her lips.

"You were the one in the car that hit Eddy last night, weren't you?"

Malone smiled. "It's a shame he left a nasty little dent

in my fender. Galin will have that fixed by tomorrow. It pays to make friends in low places, don't you think?"

"You won't get away with it."

"Yes, I will." Her smile glinted with an evil light. "I even left one of Eddy's business cards in Thomas's desk drawer in his house. So, you see, all I have to do now is kill you, kill Crane and they'll call it a murder-suicide. I'll be miles away from here and the next in line for chairman of the Appropriations Committee."

"Clever, Ann. Very clever." A male voice sounded from the kitchen door. While Malone had been bragging about her work, Congressman Crane came in the back way. He held a 9 mm pistol pointed at Congresswoman Malone. "I knew you were meeting with Jason Frazier, otherwise I wouldn't have suspected you for a moment."

"And neither will anyone else." Malone stood, her gun still aimed at TJ. "Don't try anything or she gets it."

"Now, aren't we in somewhat of a conundrum?" Crane's brow rose.

"You got that right." Malone smirked. "You shoot me, I shoot the girl and you get blamed for everything."

"Yeah, but then you lose, don't you, Ann? You won't get to be chairman. Although I don't know why you'd want it anyway. It's been nothing but a headache since Haddock died. Members of your own party don't support you when they're supposed to, do they?"

Malone smiled. "All part of my cover, sweetheart."

"Yeah." Crane snorted. "I thought you loved me."

She laughed out loud. "Not hardly. You were a means to an end. And the sex wasn't even that great."

Crane's lips pressed together. "You know I can't let you go."

"You won't shoot me. You don't have it in you."

The gun in Crane's hand exploded.

TJ dove for the floor.

Crane's shot went wide, hitting a lampshade on an end table.

Malone turned her .38 on Crane and fired, hitting him in the gut. He staggered back, his gun falling to the floor. Congressman Crane clutched at his belly where a dark red stain spread across his starched white shirt.

TJ stumbled to her feet and charged into Malone. She tackled the woman, her momentum knocking them both off their feet.

The .38 flew from Malone's hands and skittered across the hardwood floor, coming to rest by the front door.

When her shoulder made contact with the ground, TJ's world went fuzzy.

Malone scrambled to her feet and dove for the gun. Then as if in slow motion, the world erupted. The front door slammed open, hitting the wall so hard the glass in it shattered.

Sean MacNeal leaped through, his Glock at the ready.

"Oh good, the cavalry has arrived." TJ laid her head back on the floor and sighed, letting the dark haze creep closer around her until it consumed her.

HIS HEART POUNDING inside his chest, Sean scanned the room. Crane leaned against a wall, his hand to his bleeding belly. TJ lay on the floor, her eyes closed, and Ann Malone was doing a low crawl toward him, scrambling on hands and knees.

When she reached for the .38 at his feet, Sean stepped on it and aimed his weapon at the woman. "Don't." He bent, scooped the weapon up and dropped it into his pocket.

Ann Malone looked up at him, her eyes filling with tears. "But you don't understand. He tried to kill me. Thomas Crane is a mad man, a murderer." She staggered to her feet, her face a study of terror. "He killed Ms. Barton and he tried to kill me."

The world fell out from under Sean. Killed TJ?

When Ann made as if to throw herself at him, Sean pointed the gun at her chest. "Get back or I'll shoot."

"Shoot her." Crane's voice was weak and gravelly. "She's the one who shot TJ and me. She's the devil."

"You can't believe him, John. Crane was responsible for the bombing in Dindi. He wanted the oil all to himself." Ann's eyes widened. "It's true. Don't you believe me?"

Sean eased around Malone, keeping the gun leveled at her chest. Then he squatted beside TJ. "Just keep your hands where I can see them." With his gaze trained on Malone and Crane, he felt TJ's neck for a pulse. He didn't breathe for the full minute it took to find a weak heartbeat beneath her warm skin. Her shoulder was a bloody mess and her face pale, but she was still alive.

Then her eyelids fluttered open. "Sean?"

"Yeah, baby."

"She did it all." TJ's voice was a whisper of her normal strong tones.

Sean's chest tightened. "I know."

"She's crazy from loss of blood," Malone said. "She doesn't know what she's saying." The congresswoman

backed toward Crane. "He did it! Thomas was responsible for everything." Then she dove for Crane's 9 mm.
When she rolled to her feet she aimed the gun at Sean.

But not before Sean fired off a round, hitting Malone
in her right shoulder.

The bullet blasted into her, knocking her backward.
She screamed and hit the floor flat on her back, the gun
slipping from her fingers. The weapon clattered against
the floor. Ann Malone moaned and tried to rise, falling
back, her navy-blue silk pantsuit ripped and bloody, her
hair a tousled mess.

Footsteps pounded on the decking outside the door
and Tazer leaped through the door, her gun drawn. She
was followed by Royce, Valdez and Kat.

Tazer hurried to Ann Malone while Royce crossed
over to Congressman Crane, both administering first
aid. Valdez was on his cell phone with the state police
requesting ambulances and a helicopter.

Sean holstered his pistol and knelt beside TJ, gently
opening her shirt to get to the injured shoulder.

"How's TJ?" Royce asked as he calmed Crane.

"She's lost a lot of blood." Sean ripped the buttons
from his pinpoint oxford cloth shirt, stripped it off and
pulled his white T-shirt over his head. After folding it into
a tight square, he pressed the shirt against TJ's injury.

Kat laid a hand on Sean's shoulder. "Is she going to
be all right?"

"Damned right she is." With one hand he kept pressure
on the wound. He grabbed TJ's slim hand with the other
and lifted it to his face. "I love her. She'd better be okay."

"I thought you didn't believe in love?" Kat said. "It
makes you lose focus."

"I was wrong." He stared down at TJ. "I've never seen more clearly."

"Is that so?" Although her eyes remained closed, TJ's mouth moved and her words came out barely above a whisper.

"Yes, ma'am." Sean carried her hand to his lips. "If you'd hurry up and get better, I'll prove it to you."

Her eyelids flickered open and she smiled. "I'm feeling better already."

Epilogue

When Sean strode into her hospital room the next morning, TJ pushed herself up against the pillows. She hadn't seen him since the police arrived and they'd taken her away in an ambulance.

Had she imagined that he'd said he loved her? Was it all part of a dream induced by pain and loss of blood?

Her heart thumped against her rib cage. She'd refused the painkillers they'd prescribed for her earlier, wanting a clear head for when she next saw Sean. They had a lot to discuss.

Sean smiled. "How's that shoulder?"

"It'll heal." She didn't want to talk about her shoulder. It throbbed to the rhythm of her heartbeat, but she ignored it. "I hear Malone will survive."

"Yeah. The police have all the evidence they need. She should be spending her next few terms in jail, if not the rest of her life."

"Good." TJ nodded. "Now that she'll be behind bars, the rest of us can get on with our lives."

Sean stood beside her bed and lifted her hand. "Speaking of which, I spoke with Gordon. Seems you're a hero in the office. They can't wait for you to get back."

"Really?" Her gaze focused on Sean's long, tapered fingers. The thought of going back to work in the Rayburn Building was the furthest thing from TJ's mind. With Sean holding her hand, her breathing had become an issue and she fought to find the words to broach the subject of their future. Did they even have a future together?

Sean squeezed her fingers and sat on the edge of her bed, his thigh resting against hers. "That's what I wanted to talk to you about."

TJ gave a nervous laugh. "Good, because that's what I wanted to discuss with you."

"After all that's happened, you've made me realize how important it is to grab for happiness when you can."

"I did that?"

He lifted her fingers to his lips and pressed a kiss to them. "Yes, you did, and I want to be a part of your life. If you decide to go back to work at the Rayburn Building, I'll be here in the city when I'm not on assignment. I'd like to see you."

Hope filled her. "Like a date?"

"No."

"No?"

"I was thinking of something a little more permanent." He held her hand and stared into her eyes. "Tessa Janine Barton, will you marry me?"

As her heart overflowed with love, her eyes filled with moisture.

Sean leaned close and brushed a tear from her cheek. "I hope that's a good sign."

"It is." She laughed and scrubbed the tears from her eyes. "Just like any girl, I had dreams of being proposed to by a handsome man, just not in a hospital bed, wearing a hospital gown, with my hair a mess." Happiness choked off her words and more tears followed.

"You're beautiful no matter what you're wearing, and stubborn and brave." Sean snatched a tissue from the box by her bed and dabbed at her cheeks. "You do realize that you didn't answer my question, don't you?"

"Yes!" She leaned into his arms, forgetful of her wounds, intent on being close to the man she loved.

Sean held her, careful not to jostle her bandaged shoulder. He cupped her face and stared down into her watery eyes. "I love you, Tessa."

"I love you, too." Her lips met his in a hungry kiss, her body warming to his touch.

When they broke apart, Sean brushed her hair back from her forehead. "One other thing. How much do you like your job?"

TJ stared at him for a moment, digesting the change of subject. Over the past few days, she'd been thinking through her work at the Rayburn Building and she really didn't look forward to going back. "It's okay, I guess. Why?"

"I had a long talk with Royce. He wants you to come to work for the S.O.S."

"Me?" She stared at him. Of all the things he could have said, she never expected that.

"Yeah, you." Sean smiled. "He was impressed with your ability to hold it all together, even under the gun. With your background in the FBI, he thinks you'll make a great addition to the team."

Work as an S.O.S. agent? The thought took root and blossomed. She'd love it. "Are you sure?"

He nodded. "Absolutely."

Sean slid an arm around TJ and pulled her close. "Now hurry up and get better. We have our first assignment starting two weeks from today. Think you'll be up to it?"

"You bet." TJ rolled her shoulder, wincing only a little.

Sean frowned. "Are you sure?"

TJ grinned. "Absolutely."

"Good. And pack a bag for a couple weeks. We're going to Europe."

Bailey DelMonico has finally
gotten her life on track, and is
passionate about her recent career
change. Nothing will stand in the way
of her becoming a doctor...that is,
until she's paired with the sharp-tongued
Dr. Ivan Munro.

Watch the sparks fly in

Doctor in
the House

by *USA TODAY* Bestselling Author

Marie Ferrarella

Available September 2007

Intrigued? Read more at
TheNextNovel.com

HARLEQUIN®
Next™

HN88141

ATHENA FORCE

**Heart-pounding romance
and thrilling adventure.**

A deadly masquerade

As an undercover asset for the FBI, mafia princess
Sasha Bracciali can deceive and improvise at a
moment's notice. But when she's cut off from
everything she knows, including her FBI-agent
lover, Sasha realizes her deceptions have masked
a painful truth: she doesn't know whom to trust.
If she doesn't figure it out quickly, her most
ambitious charade will also be her last.

Look for

CHARADE
by *Kate Donovan*

*Available in October
wherever you buy books.*

HARLEQUIN®

Mediterranean NIGHTS™

Sail aboard the luxurious Alexandra's Dream *and experience glamour, romance, mystery and revenge!*

Coming in October 2007...

AN AFFAIR TO REMEMBER

by

Karen Kendall

When Captain Nikolas Pappas first fell in love with Helena Stamos, he was a penniless deckhand and she was the daughter of a shipping magnate. But he's never forgiven himself for the way he left her—and fifteen years later, he's determined to win her back.

Though the attraction is still there, Helena is hesitant to get involved. Nick left her once...what's to stop him from doing it again?

REQUEST YOUR FREE BOOKS!

2 FREE NOVELS PLUS 2 FREE GIFTS!

HARLEQUIN®

INTRIGUE®

Breathtaking Romantic Suspense

YES! Please send me 2 FREE Harlequin Intrigue® novels and my 2 FREE gifts. After receiving them, if I don't wish to receive any more books, I can return the shipping statement marked "cancel." If I don't cancel, I will receive 6 brand-new novels every month and be billed just $4.24 per book in the U.S., or $4.99 per book in Canada, plus 25¢ shipping and handling per book and applicable taxes, if any*. That's a savings of close to 15% off the cover price! I understand that accepting the 2 free books and gifts places me under no obligation to buy anything. I can always return a shipment and cancel at any time. Even if I never buy another book from Harlequin, the two free books and gifts are mine to keep forever.

182 HDN EEZ7   382 HDN EEZK

Name	(PLEASE PRINT)	
Address		Apt. #
City	State/Prov.	Zip/Postal Code

Signature (if under 18, a parent or guardian must sign)

Mail to the **Harlequin Reader Service®:**
IN U.S.A.: P.O. Box 1867, Buffalo, NY 14240-1867
IN CANADA: P.O. Box 609, Fort Erie, Ontario L2A 5X3

Not valid to current Harlequin Intrigue subscribers.

Want to try two free books from another line?
Call 1-800-873-8635 or visit www.morefreebooks.com.

* Terms and prices subject to change without notice. NY residents add applicable sales tax. Canadian residents will be charged applicable provincial taxes and GST. This offer is limited to one order per household. All orders subject to approval. Credit or debit balances in a customer's account(s) may be offset by any other outstanding balance owed by or to the customer. Please allow 4 to 6 weeks for delivery.

Your Privacy: Harlequin is committed to protecting your privacy. Our Privacy Policy is available online at www.eHarlequin.com or upon request from the Reader Service. From time to time we make our lists of customers available to reputable firms who may have a product or service of interest to you. If you would prefer we not share your name and address, please check here. ☐

nocturne™

Look for

NIGHT MISCHIEF

by

NINA BRUHNS

Lady Dawn Maybank's worst nightmare
is realized when she accidentally conjures
a demon of vengeance, Galen McManus. What
she doesn't realize is that Galen plans to teach
her a lesson in love—one she'll never forget....

DARK ENCHANTMENTS
▲

Available October wherever you buy books.

*Don't miss the last installment of Dark Enchantments,
SAVING DESTINY by Pat White, available November.*

Silhouette®

Desire

There was only one man for the job—
an impossible-to-resist maverick
she knew she didn't dare fall for.

MAVERICK
(#1827)

BY *NEW YORK TIMES*
BESTSELLING AUTHOR
JOAN HOHL

"Will You Do It for One Million Dollars?"

Any other time, Tanner Wolfe would have balked at being
hired by a woman. Yet Brianna Stewart was desperate to
engage the infamous bounty hunter. The price was just
high enough to gain Tanner's interest…Brianna's beauty
definitely strong enough to keep it. But he wasn't about
to allow her to tag along on his mission. He worked
alone. Always had. Always would. However, he'd never
confronted a more determined client than Brianna. She
wasn't taking no for an answer—not about anything.

Perhaps a million-dollar bounty was not the only thing
this maverick was about to gain….

Look for MAVERICK

Available October 2007 wherever you buy books.

Silhouette® Romantic SUSPENSE

*Sparked by Danger,
Fueled by Passion.*

When evidence is found that Mallory Dawes
intends to sell the personal financial information
of government employees to "the Russian,"
OMEGA engages undercover agent Cutter Smith.
Tailing her all the way to France, Cutter is
fighting a growing attraction to Mallory while at
the same time having to determine her connection
to "the Russian." Is Mallory really the mouse in
this game of cat and mouse?

Look for

Stranded with a Spy

by *USA TODAY* bestselling author

Merline Lovelace

October 2007.

Also available October wherever you buy books:

BULLETPROOF MARRIAGE *(Mission: Impassioned)*
by Karen Whiddon

A HERO'S REDEMPTION *(Haven)* by Suzanne McMinn

TOUCHED BY FIRE by Elizabeth Sinclair

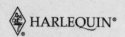

COMING NEXT MONTH

www.eHarlequin.com

HICNM0907